Praise for Kate Hoffmann's The Mighty Quinns

"*The Mighty Quinns: Thom* does a great job of showing the characters' flaws, and their redemptive journey makes the love story that much more potent."
—*RT Book Reviews*

"[Kate] Hoffmann always brings a strong story to the table with The Mighty Quinns, and this is one of her best."
—*RT Book Reviews* on *The Mighty Quinns: Eli*

"[Hoffmann's] characters are well written and real. *The Mighty Quinns: Eli* is a recommended read for lovers of the Quinn family, lovers of the outdoors and lovers of a sensitive man."
—*Harlequin Junkie*

"The [Aileen Quinn storyline] ends as it began: with strong storytelling and compelling, tender characters who make for a deeply satisfying read."
—*RT Book Reviews* on *The Mighty Quinns: Mac*

"A winning combination of exciting adventure and romance... This is a sweet and sexy read that kept me entertained from start to finish."
—*Harlequin Junkie* on *The Mighty Quinns: Malcolm*

"This is a fast read that is hard to tear the eyes from. Once I picked it up I couldn't put it down."
—*Fresh Fiction* on *The Mighty Quinns: Dermot*

Dear Reader,

It's hard to believe, but this title, *The Mighty Quinns: Jamie*, is my 90th story for Harlequin. I've come such a long way from that first novel.

I've worked with many different editors on books for many Harlequin series, including Temptation, Love & Laughter and Blaze, as well as various miniseries and novellas. I've scoured the world for Quinns, creating a family saga that is currently thirty-seven books long.

Is this the last of the Quinns? It's hard to say. But I will be working on some exciting new projects in the future, so be sure to stay tuned.

Happy reading,

Kate Hoffmann

Kate Hoffmann

The Mighty Quinns: Jamie

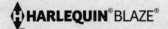

HARLEQUIN® BLAZE®

Recycling programs
for this product may
not exist in your area.

ISBN-13: 978-0-373-79953-4

The Mighty Quinns: Jamie

Copyright © 2017 by Peggy A. Hoffmann

This edition published by arrangement with Harlequin Books S.A.

For questions and comments about the quality of this book, please contact us at CustomerService@Harlequin.com.

Printed in U.S.A.

Kate Hoffmann's first book was published by Harlequin in 1993 and in the twenty-some years since, she has written ninety stories for the publisher. When she isn't writing, she enjoys genealogy, golfing and directing student theater productions. She lives in southeastern Wisconsin with her two cats, Winnie and Gracie.

Books by Kate Hoffmann

Harlequin Blaze

Seducing the Marine
Compromising Positions

The Mighty Quinns

The Mighty Quinns: Dex
The Mighty Quinns: Malcolm
The Mighty Quinns: Rogan
The Mighty Quinns: Ryan
The Mighty Quinns: Eli
The Mighty Quinns: Devin
The Mighty Quinns: Mac
The Mighty Quinns: Thom
The Mighty Quinns: Tristan

To get the inside scoop on Harlequin Blaze and its talented writers, visit Facebook.com/BlazeAuthors.

All backlist available in ebook format.

Visit the Author Profile page at Harlequin.com for more titles.

To Malle Vallik,

who took a chance on me and gave me my first Harlequin contract.

Number 90 is for you!

Prologue

"WHAT DOES IT MEAN?" Jamie Quinn asked, staring at the bright yellow card stapled to the front door of their house on Downey Street in Minneapolis.

"It's an eviction notice," Thom said. His older brother reached for the shiny new padlock that had been attached to the door, preventing them from entering. A shiver of dread rattled through Jamie's body, but he clenched his teeth and ignored it. He'd learned to control his deepest fears. He could be as strong as his older brothers if he had to be.

"How can they evict us?" Tristan asked. "We paid the rent last month."

"Yeah, but we were already five months behind," Thom explained.

"All our stuff is inside. How are we going to get it?"

"We'll break in," Thom said. "But we'll wait until it gets dark. There's a broken window in the basement that Jamie can squeeze through. Until then, we're going to have to find a place to sleep for the night."

The trio walked off the crumbling porch and headed down the street.

It wasn't fair, Jamie thought to himself. Grown-ups could find a job and pay for the rent. But how were kids supposed to have a home if they couldn't have a job?

He'd tried to find a way to make money. He'd asked if he could deliver newspapers and they'd said he was too young. And when he'd tried to carry groceries for tips, the owner of the store had chased him away. And most of the neighbors were too poor to pay him to walk their dogs.

"If we're not at the house, how is Ma going to find us when she gets out?" Tris asked.

Their mother had been caught shoplifting last month and was serving three months in the county jail. Somehow, Social Services had lost their address and the boys had been on their own since then. Now, with the eviction, their lives had been turned upside down all over again. They were on the street and they were vulnerable.

"We could sleep in my fort," Jamie suggested.

"Your fort? Since when do you have a fort?" Tristan asked.

Jamie shrugged. "Since I discovered it last month. I've been collecting some stuff. It's warm and private and we can all sleep there. No one would know."

Thom studied him for a long moment. "You wanna show us where this fort is?"

"It's supposed to be secret," Jamie said as he led them around to the back of the house. "So you guys have to swear that you'll never tell anyone else."

"Who are we going to tell?" Tristan asked.

Jamie led them through a maze of alleyways, keeping his eye out for anyone who might see them pass. When he was certain they weren't being followed, he back-tracked until they came to a ramshackle garage about a block from their house. "You stay here," he ordered his two older brothers. "Don't let anyone see you. I'll show you how to get in and then you follow me."

Jamie used a garbage bin to boost himself up onto the roof. Scrambling up the slope, he was careful not to slip on the patches of unmelted snow on the old shingles. When he reached the peak, he hung over the edge and kicked open an old window. Then, with one swing, he landed lightly on the sill. A few seconds later he was inside, motioning for his brother Tris to follow his lead.

When all three brothers were in, Jamie shut the window, pulled a curtain over it and reached for the light. In an instant, the loft of the old garage was illuminated, revealing a tidy array of cardboard boxes and crates. Jamie smiled to himself.

Inside, the garage was state-of-the-art. The owner had camouflaged his sleek workshop beneath flaking paint and crumbling shingles. Jamie walked over to the edge of the loft. "The guy keeps the place heated in the winter. And there's water and electricity and a refrigerator."

"Wow, look at this place," Tris murmured. "It's nicer than our house."

"If he takes care of his cars this way, you gotta wonder how he treats his kids," Thom said. He peered over the railing at the pair of vehicles, hidden beneath canvas covers. "What kind of cars does he have?"

Jamie shrugged. "I don't know. Something foreign."

"What if he comes?" Tris asked.

"He only comes on the weekends, during the day. And all the lights turn on as soon as he opens the door, so he wouldn't notice if we were here." Jamie moved over to the far wall. "I found some old blankets. And I've got books. And he even has a television downstairs."

Thom reached out and pulled Jamie into a fierce hug. "You did great, little brother. We'll stay here for now. When Ma gets out of jail, we can find a new place."

Jamie smiled to himself. It wasn't often his brothers gave him credit for doing something useful. He was usually the one dependent on them for all of life's necessities. But this time he'd managed to find them a temporary home—a place that was safe and warm and comfortable.

Someday, when he was older and had a job, he could use his money to help people who didn't have a home. He could put a home in the loft of every garage in the neighborhood so there would always be places to live.

Or he could buy some wood and build houses that no one could take away. There would be no landlords and no rent, and absolutely no evictions. Everyone would be safe and warm, and Social Services would never come to take any kids from their parents.

His teachers always told him that everyone should have a dream. He'd always thought they were talking about stuff like being an astronaut or a basketball player. Maybe it was enough to be a guy who built houses...

_1_

THERE WAS SOMETHING about the very beginning of the day that Regan Macintosh loved. That moment when the first light appeared in the eastern sky and washed away the previous day, preparing her for a completely fresh start. No worries, no disappointments. Just the possibility of a perfect day ahead of her—and perhaps the perfect photograph.

Her internal clock followed the seasons, always waking her up precisely fifteen minutes before the sun appeared on the horizon. The late September weather in Minnesota was a mix of warm and breezy days followed by chilly nights. The leaves were just beginning to turn, and flocks of geese lifted from the lake each morning and headed south.

When she spent the night at her grandmother's place on the eastern shore of Pickett's Lake, as she'd done last night, she often took advantage of the early start and got up to take a walk, her favorite camera in hand. The light was always the best in the early morning hours, and the most unexpected images could be captured when the rest of the world was still asleep.

Regan wasn't sure when she'd begun the search, but the need to find the perfect image had grown more important to her as she got older. Just once, she wanted to snap the shutter and be completely and totally satisfied with the image, no need to alter it on her computer, no regrets about how she'd framed it.

Regan dropped her camera strap over her head, then opened the door and slipped outside. She drew a deep breath of chilly morning air, the smell of the Minnesota woods and lakes filling her head. So different from the smell of her winter home in the desert of Arizona.

As she walked up to the road, a sense of anticipation built within her. A low fog hugged the floor of the forest, and in the distance, she could hear the cry of a blue jay.

Her parents and siblings had joked about her search for perfection when she was younger, teasing her about all her lists and plans. But she'd always been that way, finding something she was passionate about and then pursuing it with every ounce of her energy and every second of her time.

Her fascination with photography had grown from one of her biggest childhood obsessions—brides. It had begun when she'd first watched the wedding scene in *The Sound of Music*. After that, she wasn't happy unless she was wearing a long white gown and a veil. Sometimes they were made of clothes she'd stolen from her mother's closet, other times they were made of toilet paper or tissue paper.

Every Halloween, she wore the same costume—full bridal regalia, down to a rhinestone tiara and jeweled shoes. On her sixth birthday, she'd received a digital camera from her parents, who'd hoped she'd find a new obsession. Instead, she'd learned to use the timer and took photos of herself dressed in her bridal creations.

As she walked down the empty road now, she thought back to the carefree summers she'd spent at her grandparents' lake house. When she turned eight, she'd been allowed to ride her bike into town, and that's when she'd discovered real weddings. All summer long, beautiful brides and their handsome husbands would celebrate their wedding in the old stone chapel.

Sometimes she'd sneak in and take photos from the balcony, though most often she was forced to wait outside. But every summer, she'd fill scrapbooks full of photos, every year learning new ways to make them more beautiful.

The chapel came into view as she came around the bend, appearing out of the mist. She picked up her camera and snapped a few frames. But as she came closer, she noticed movement on the front steps—a fox sat on the top one. The fox hadn't noticed her and she slowly brought her camera up. The light was dull, but it would get better if she waited.

Slowly, step by step, she moved to a better vantage point, keeping the camera trained on the fox. As she waited for the sun, her mind spooled back to her own wedding day. She'd known Jake Lindstrom for most of her life. His family owned the huge house on the eastern shore of Pickett Lake, and their parents had socialized in the same circles in the city.

It was supposed to have been the wedding of the summer, with a huge reception planned at the local country club. She'd spent her last year of college planning every detail, and after trying on over two hundred wedding gowns, she'd finally found the perfect dress.

Everything had gone as planned until she reached the altar. That was when the man of her dreams, her fairy-tale prince, had blurted out a drunken apology before running for the door.

In that instant, every dream she had of being the perfect bride had been destroyed, along with her belief in the perfect relationship. How was it possible to love someone and then just stop? What was wrong with her that she didn't deserve the fairy-tale ending?

From that moment on, she'd kept the men in her life at a distance. She'd dated and enjoyed some passionate short-term affairs, but she'd kept her heart locked away. Most men found her approach attractive and enjoyed the no-strings sex. And though most of her lovers would have been happy to continue, Regan had always been the one to end it.

As she continued to watch the fox, Regan thought about all the photos she'd taken as a wedding photographer. People said she had a way of capturing emotion in her photographs of inanimate objects—rose petals on a white runner, a wedding program left on a church pew, a veil tossed across the back of a chair. She mixed these photos with stunning candids and beautiful portraits, capturing the day in a way that no one else could.

It was easier to believe in the fairy tale when she stood behind the camera. It was like a filter that took away the everyday realities of love and marriage and froze the moments of perfection for all time.

A soft breeze buffeted the dead leaves that covered the roadside, sending them onto the pavement in swirls of color. Suddenly, the low morning light finally broke through the trees. Horizontal shafts of illumination reflected off the moisture in the air and the colors shifted, becoming supersaturated, an emerald so vivid it seemed unreal.

She brought the camera up again and began to shoot. The fox sniffed at the wind, then flicked her tail, turning its attention to the road. Regan held her breath as she continued to shoot. It was as if the fox sensed that Regan meant no harm. In fact, she wanted her photo taken.

The sunlight moved up the facade of the chapel and had nearly covered the fox with a diffuse light. Suddenly, the fox's ears pricked up and she cocked her head. Regan let out a soft gasp as she heard the sound of singing echoing through the woods.

"Give me some men, who are stout hearted men, who will fight for the right they adore."

In a heartbeat, the fox bounded off into the woods. Regan looked up from her camera, cursing softly, as the voice grew louder. A few seconds later, she saw a runner approaching from the opposite direction. He wore running pants and trainers, but he'd removed his long-sleeved shirt and tied it around his waist. His chest was bare to the cold and gleaming with moisture.

He continued to sing the song until he caught sight

of her. Then he stopped in the middle of the road, as if he were startled to see somebody out so early in the morning. Steam seemed to swirl around his body—from the cold air meeting his warm skin—and for a moment, Regan wondered if he was real.

They stared at each other for a long moment, like predator and prey, although Regan wasn't sure which one of them was which. She wanted to scream at him and throw rocks and sticks until she punished him for ruining her photo session. But all she could manage was a frustrated shriek and a sarcastic "thank you."

She spun on her heel and started back toward her grandmother's house. The family of foxes would have been a cute photo, one that she could have turned into a postcard for the tourists who flocked to Pickett Lake every summer. Instead, some bonehead more concerned about his washboard abs and muscled calves than appreciating nature had ruined it.

A few seconds later, the runner caught up to her. "Did you just thank me?"

"I wasn't being grateful," Regan said. "You just scared away my shot."

"Your shot?"

"A fox. Sitting on the chapel steps. Perfect light."

"All the better," he said. "You might've killed me."

Regan held up her camera, waving it in his face. "Not that kind of shot. Though the way I feel right now, I could kill you," she said. "It was going to be a beautiful picture, and you ruined it with that ridiculous song."

"You know that song?"

"My grandfather used to sing it every year when we

dragged the dock down to the water." Regan couldn't help but smile at the memory of all the grandchildren lined up on either side and marching the heavy wooden structure down to the water. It was an annual rite of passage. No one was allowed to swim in the lake until the dock was in.

"Well then, I suppose I do owe you an apology. I'm sorry for ruining your shot," he said. "And I guess if you're determined to shoot me there's nothing I can do about it."

He ran a few steps ahead of her, then turned to face her, jogging backward and holding his arms out. "Go ahead, I'm ready to accept my punishment."

Regan couldn't help but smile again. She'd been so angry with him just a few moments ago and now he'd made her smile. Who was this man?

She raised her camera and snapped a few frames. He clutched his chest and stumbled slightly. "I suppose I deserve that."

Regan raised her camera again, this time focusing on his face. He continued to increase the distance between them as she continued to shoot, and when she pulled the camera down, he was twenty yards away. She opened her mouth, ready to ask him to stop. She wanted to know more about him, where he came from, what he was doing on the road so early in the morning. But in the end, she let him escape. He finally faced forward and continued down the road, singing the song boisterously.

Regan quickly grabbed a few shots of his retreat, then stood in the middle of the road and listened to the last echo of his voice. She'd had a lot of strange encounters on her early morning walks, mostly with wild animals. She could say with complete confidence, though, that she'd never had an encounter with such a handsome man.

She realized it had been a long time since she'd enjoyed being with a sexy man. And she had a few months before she headed to Arizona for the winter. Regan glanced at her watch. If he ran on a regular schedule, she might catch him out here again tomorrow morning. Then she might be able to find out where he lived and who he was. And she wouldn't be so…so tongue-tied.

Regan hurried back to the house, slipping silently inside and heading for the kitchen. She pulled the data stick out of her camera and plugged it into the laptop she'd left on the kitchen counter the night before. Tapping her finger impatiently, Regan waited while the images loaded. The instant they had, she brought up the pictures of the stranger.

Clicking on his face in the first one, she enlarged the photo until she could see every detail. Her breath caught in her throat as she stared into his deep blue eyes. "Oh, my," she murmured, pressing her hand to her chest. Her heart was pounding beneath her palm and she tried to draw a deep breath again.

The photo showed the mist and the sunlight filtering through the trees and catching the sheen of moisture on his face and body. It all combined to produce a beautiful image of an incredibly stunning man. Regan swallowed hard as she reached out to touch her computer screen.

In the image, he was holding his arms out, chal-

lenging her to shoot. His smile was playful, teasing…
as if he knew exactly how to make her laugh. And she
had laughed.

Handsome and sexy and funny. Exactly what she
looked for in a man. Since Jake, she didn't need to worry
about anything else—like fidelity or honesty or loyalty.
She never allowed her relationships to reach the point
where those qualities made a difference. She wasn't
looking for Prince Charming anymore. But that didn't
mean she'd didn't want a man in her bed every now
and then.

She had twenty-four hours. Then she'd walk the road
again and hope that this charming, sexy guy was a crea-
ture of habit.

A BRISK BREEZE sent leaves skittering across the main
street of the small town of Pickett Lake. Jamie Quinn
got out of his pickup and looked both ways before jogging to the opposite sidewalk. He climbed the front
steps of the old hardware store, reaching into his jacket
pocket for the business card of a local real estate agent.

He'd arrived in town yesterday evening, taking a
room at a local motel. After a decent night's sleep, a
great morning run, an odd encounter with a feisty photographer and a hearty breakfast, he was ready to get
down to business.

Jamie was on a strict schedule that didn't allow for
any flexibility. He had just two more weeks to find a
piece of land before he was scheduled to start building
his first modular home. After that, every hour would
be accounted for on a time sheet that would be ana-

lyzed and discussed between him and his two business partners.

He stepped inside the store, the old wood floors creaking beneath his feet as he searched for a friendly face. He noticed that the other patrons were simply piling their purchases on the counter, then going back through the aisles to fetch the additional items they needed.

An elderly man nodded at him. "Can I help you find anything, sir?"

"I'm looking for Walt Murphy," Jamie said.

"Can I tell him what it's about?"

"I'm Jamie Quinn. I called him yesterday. I'm looking to lease a lot with lake frontage."

"You want to rent a piece of property?" the man asked.

"No, just the land…it's kind of a complicated story. Can you get Walt?"

"He's in the back. Let me fetch him for you," the clerk said.

The idea for Habikit had come a few years ago, as he and two friends had gone out for beers after a hockey game. Sam Fraley, an architect, and Rick Santino, a construction contractor, had been arguing about the "tiny house" movement and the potential effects it could have on the construction industry.

But Jamie had argued that it offered intriguing possibilities to provide prefabricated homes to the homeless. There'd been a time in his life when safe and warm housing wasn't always a given, and he'd been searching for the opportunity to do something to help others in the same situation.

And so the Habikit was born. The materials for a complete two-hundred-square-foot home would be packed in a box and shipped to wherever it was needed. They'd designed each kit to be a module that could be expanded to make a larger home for a reasonable price. Sam and Rick and Jamie worked to make the kit simple to construct, with a minimum of tools and equipment. They'd also focused on making the kits "green" and using recycled materials whenever possible, achieving a nearly net-zero carbon footprint.

It had been a labor of love for the three of them, and after a year of designing, they'd built their first module together, donating it to a homeless housing project in Minneapolis. The tiny home had garnered a multitude of awards, along with the interest of investors. But those investors were looking for proof that Jamie and his friends could make a profit. So they'd devised phase two—using the concept to build a vacation home.

The sale of modular vacation homes would provide a major source of funding for the nonprofit homeless project. But it wasn't enough to make up a brochure with an illustration. Investors wanted to see a real home built in a natural setting and they were in danger of losing their most important investor if the project wasn't finished within a month.

So Jamie had set out to lease a piece of waterfront property. Once he'd obtained the proper permits, he'd build Habikit's first multi-module home, documenting it along the way with photos and videos for the instruction manual.

"Excuse me? Can you help me?"

Jamie turned to find an elderly woman standing behind him. Her pale blond hair was swept into a tidy knot and her smooth skin made it impossible to guess her age. She wore a canvas coat, khakis and knee-high wellies.

"I'm sorry," he said. "I don't work here."

She smiled, her blue eyes twinkling. "I don't need your expertise. I just need your eyes. You wouldn't think I'd have to carry a magnifying glass around with me, but I can't read the directions."

"I can help you out with that," Jamie said, taking the package of glue from her fingers. He read off the instructions, and when the woman realized it wasn't what she was looking for, he helped her find an epoxy that would work better.

"Thank you for your help."

"I was happy to come to your rescue, madam," Jamie said.

She held out her hand. "Celia Macintosh," she said. "And what's your name, young man?"

"James Quinn. But everyone calls me Jamie," he said.

"Jamie, I couldn't help but overhear," she said. "You're looking to lease some land?"

"I am," Jamie said. "And it has to have lake frontage. It's hard to find someone willing to rent a piece of lake property. Especially for the price I can pay."

"Mr. Quinn?"

Jamie turned to see a middle-aged man approach. He

was dressed in a comfortable sport coat and a neatly pressed shirt. His graying hair was shaggy and he looked like he'd been taking a nap. "Mr. Murphy?"

The real estate broker held out his hand. "Walt Murphy. What can I do for you?"

"Nothing," Celia said. "Mr. Quinn doesn't need your help anymore." She cleared her throat. "As I was saying, Mr. Quinn, I have a lovely little spot that I might be interested in leasing. To the right person."

"Since when do you have land to lease, Miss Celia?" Walt asked.

"Never you mind." She gave Jamie a coy smile. "Come along, Mr. Quinn, we have business to discuss." She handed the package of glue to Walt. "Walter, say hello to your mother for me. And get yourself a haircut!"

"Miss Celia, I seem to recall that your property is held in a trust. You aren't authorized to lease it to a third party," Walt said. "Maybe Mr. Quinn should talk to your granddaughter before you make any decisions. Miss Regan knows best."

"Don't be ridiculous," Celia said. "I can make these decisions on my own. I don't need Regan's help. And I do have property of my own. I have Maple Point."

Walt frowned. "You'd consider selling the point? But I thought you'd—"

"Walt, you know there's no decent property left on the lake. Unless you were going to try to sell that raggedy little piece of swampland that you own over on the western shore." Celia turned to Jamie. "Why don't we go look at my property?"

"All right," Jamie said.

As they started toward the door, Walt grabbed Jamie's arm. "Everyone around town loves Miss Celia. We look out for each other here in Pickett Lake. If you do anything to hurt her, if you take advantage of her, the whole town will kick your ass."

"I appreciate the warning," Jamie said. "I have a grandmother who I care very much for and if it were her, I would have the same concerns as you do."

Though his grandmother had appeared in their lives too late to save them from most of their troubles, she had provided a steadying influence to Jamie, as the youngest in the family, during his high school years.

"Well, good, I'm glad we got that cleared up," Walt said.

Jamie followed Celia out to the street. She withdrew a pair of leather gloves from her pocket, then pointed to a pale yellow Mercedes parked down the street. "Tell me, Mr. Quinn, what do you intend to build on my land? A nice little summer cottage for your wife and children?"

Jamie chuckled. "No," he said. "I don't have a wife. Or children."

"Really?" She smiled. "I'm surprised. Why is that? You seem like a very nice man. Handsome. Successful."

"How do you know that?"

"You're dressed well. And you're interested in my property, which won't come cheap."

"I'm planning to build a model home, a modular design that my company produces. We'll use the home for photos and to show investors. And when we don't need it any longer, in three or four years, we'll take it down and return the land to its original state."

"I could lease you the land," she said. "But what if I wanted to keep the cottage? Maybe you could just leave it where it was?"

"You're a very shrewd woman, Miss Celia."

"I am."

Jamie helped her into her car, then jogged across the street to his pickup. He made a U-turn and tucked his truck in behind the Mercedes, following her down the main street and along to Shore Road, where they maintained a lazy pace through the tight curves that cut through the thick woods.

He recognized the route. It had been the same path he'd taken that morning on his jog. His mind flashed back to his encounter with the brash but beautiful photographer.

He'd meant to ask about her around town, see if anyone knew who she was. But until now, he hadn't been sure he'd be staying in Pickett Lake. The resort community was quite close to Minneapolis, which made it an ideal location to build the model quickly. But it was also a small town, and he'd been aware that the chances of finding available and affordable land he could lease would be small. Running into Celia had been a godsend. And if he did secure a piece of property here, maybe he could get to know the intriguing photographer.

He remembered that she was beautiful, and that the color of her eyes had been mesmerizing—a deep, emerald green. And her voice had been soft and melodic, as if she could persuade anyone she met to do her bidding.

Even now, he could imagine that voice, teasing at his ear, saying his name, convincing him to let down his guard, to surrender to his—

Jamie stopped himself. This was crazy. He hadn't asked the woman's name because he'd thought he was leaving town. Besides, he was the kind of guy who didn't like to be tied down. He made it a point to avoid messy romances. He preferred women who wanted nothing more than a night or two of physical pleasure with long intervals between. But this woman was far too beautiful to settle for no-strings sex. He could imagine that she had men hanging on her every word, men lining up to date her. Men ready to pledge their lives to her.

Hell, she was probably married. Or involved. Why hadn't he lingered a bit longer and introduced himself?

The brake lights on the old Mercedes flashed and Celia quickly slowed the car and pulled it into a narrow paved driveway, not far from where he'd met the photographer. Maybe Celia knew who she was. Jamie made a mental note to ask her just as soon as it wouldn't seem strange.

The house, or more accurately, the lodge, was made of logs and set in a wide clearing that overlooked the lake. Though he knew there were neighbors around, the trees were so thick that it gave the illusion of complete solitude and privacy.

Celia pulled to a stop in the wide circle drive, then elegantly stepped from the car, smoothing her hands over her hair. Jamie had noticed her air of wealth in the hardware store, but after seeing her house, it was clear that Celia didn't need the income from her land to be financially secure.

Jamie hopped out of the truck and strolled over to stand next to her. "This is quite a place," he said.

"My late husband, Kenneth, built it so we could have the whole family here during the summers," she explained. "But everyone has gone off in different directions, and my husband passed two years ago. The only time the house is full is at Thanksgiving, Christmas and on my birthday in July."

"How many children do you have?" Jamie asked.

"I have five children and seventeen grandchildren," Celia said. "Let's walk out to the point first, and I'll show you the land."

They walked around the house to a wide stone terrace that offered a picturesque view of the lake. A second-story deck surrounded the back of the house and stairs led up to a wall of windows. "This is beautiful," Jamie said. "Like paradise."

"I used to think so. Now it's just a big, empty house filled with memories."

Jamie pointed to a small building close to the lake. "Is that a boathouse?"

"No, that's a guest cabin. It was on the property when we bought it. My husband and I lived there while we were building the lodge."

"I need a place to stay while I'm building the model," he said. "Would you consider renting the cabin?"

"I suppose I could. The furnace isn't working and the plumbing is turned off. But I could probably get it ready. When would you want to move in?"

"Well, I have to get the permits to start building, and that could take a few weeks. But I have to finish before the end of October, or the weather is going to get bad and our investors might get antsy. So I'd probably be back in mid-October?" He laughed. "But I haven't even seen the point yet. Maybe we should start with that."

As they walked along the lakeshore, Jamie explained the goals of his company, the need for simple ways to provide housing for the homeless and how lake cottages would help fund their altruistic aims.

Celia listened intently, asking questions along the way. As he explained, her enthusiasm for the project seemed to grow.

Once they arrived at the point, Jamie could tell it would be perfect. Now all they needed to do was come to terms and hope her family didn't object.

2

REGAN FUSSED WITH the folds of the pretty crocheted baby blanket, then stepped back to check the composition of the photo.

A local family had booked her new baby package and she'd spent the afternoon shooting the young couple and their infant daughter. They'd begun outdoors among the bright colors of fall, and now she was finishing up with mother and baby relaxing in a rocking chair in the nursery.

"There," she whispered. "Now, just turn your head slightly and look out the window."

Regan focused on the sleeping baby, her gaze taking in the precious details of the little girl's features—the long lashes, the tiny nose, the Cupid's bow lips. She swallowed hard as the usual flood of emotion hit her. It always did in moments like these, whenever she was shooting a baby.

After Jake, she'd given up her dreams of a fairy-tale marriage. And she was content with the decision. She couldn't imagine ever allowing herself to be that vulnerable again. But along with giving up on marriage, she'd also given up on children of her own in the near future. And occasionally that still stung.

Someday, if she still wanted a baby, she'd have one. She didn't need a husband, though she would have to find someone to donate the genetic material. But how hard could that be?

As she peered through the camera, her mind drifted back to the man she'd met on the road a few weeks ago. Whenever she had a spare moment, she couldn't help but think about him. He'd been just about the most exciting thing to happen in her life in the past year.

She'd asked around town, a few discreet questions here and there, but no one had heard of any strangers staying in town. She'd thought he might be the new owner of the Hamill cottage, about a quarter mile down the road from her grandmother's. The place had sold recently and he'd come from that direction. Her grandmother would have known the man if he'd been her new neighbor. She made it a point to acquaint herself with everyone who lived in Pickett Lake.

But it was sometimes best for Regan to keep her personal life to herself. Ceci had a tendency to become too invested in whomever she saw as potential husband material for Regan. The moment Regan showed interest in a man, her grandmother began preparing the guest list for the wedding. No matter how many times she'd explained that she wasn't planning on ever getting engaged again, Ceci tried to convince her to give love just one more chance.

She snapped off a few more shots of the mother and child, then moved to a new angle, clicking the shutter until she was satisfied she had what she needed. "We're done," Regan said. as she placed the lens cap back on her camera.

Amy Farrell slowly stood, taking care not to wake her baby. "Won't you please give me a peek?"

Regan shook her head, moving around the nursery and searching for items that would make good still-life shots. "No. I never let anyone look. It's why you hired me. I find the best shots and I'll make them beautiful. I promise you won't be disappointed."

Amy smiled. "All right. Well, thank you. And call me when they're ready. We want to pick one for our Christmas card."

Amy wandered out of the nursery, her daughter still asleep in her arms, and Regan packed up her things. As she hauled her gear out to her car, she pulled her phone from her jacket pocket.

Her grandmother had called twice over the last few days to invite Regan to dinner. She'd texted her grandmother that she was too busy editing recent wedding shoots, but would come just as soon as she had a free evening.

Though she had a small apartment above her storefront in town, Regan spent about a third of her nights at her grandmother's. She knew how lonely Ceci got and how much she enjoyed cooking for her, so whenever she had a break from work, she'd make the short drive to the lodge.

Regan usually tried to have dinner with her grandmother at least twice a week, but with her fall wedding schedule and a trip to New York a couple weeks ago for an industry show, it had been nearly three weeks. When she got inside her car, she dialed her grandmother's number.

She had a few days before she needed to go through the photos from the baby shoot. And the wedding she'd been scheduled to photograph on the weekend had been canceled last month.

Ceci's voice mail picked up and Regan waited to speak.

"Hi, Nana, it's Regan. I just wanted to say that I'm finally free for dinner tonight. I just have to make a quick stop at the hardware store to pick up batteries for my camera and then I'll be right over. Call me back if you need anything from the store and I can grab it. See you soon. Love you."

Regan turned the car in the direction of the hardware store. She was cutting it close; Walt Murphy closed his doors at exactly 5:00 p.m. and she had three minutes to get the special batteries he carried for her equipment.

She pulled up in front of the store just as he was coming out. "Thank God you're still open," she cried.

Walt chuckled and pointed to the door he'd just closed. "We'll be open at eight tomorrow morning."

"I just need a few of those cadmium batteries. They don't carry them at the grocery store and I wanted to get some sunrise shots tomorrow for the fire department calendar."

"Well, as a volunteer fireman, I suppose I'll have to make an exception." Walt reopened the door. "I'm glad you stopped by. I wanted to talk to you about your grandmother."

"My grandmother?"

"Yes," Walt said, holding the door open for her. "She was in the store a few weeks ago and she happened to meet this stranger named Quinn. He'd stopped by to see me, looking for a piece of land to build on. Next thing I know, she's offering him Maple Point."

Regan gasped. "*Our* Maple Point?"

"Yep. I figured she can't go leasing or selling land that's in a trust, but then I found out that piece of land belongs to her. She bought it herself way back when. I was gonna call you, but then I figured it wasn't my place to butt into family business."

Regan grabbed the batteries she'd come for and handed Walt enough money to cover the bill. "Thanks for telling me. I appreciate it."

"If she wants to sell Maple Point, I know I can get her top dollar if she'll let me list it."

"She won't be selling that land," she assured him.

Regan cursed beneath her breath. Since her grandfather had died, two years ago, her grandmother had been at loose ends. The family had urged Celia to sell the lodge and buy something smaller, but Celia had insisted on keeping it for the family, hoping to recreate those perfect summers of the past, the house packed full of three generations of the Macintosh family.

Since Regan was the only family member living in the area, it had become her responsibility to sort out any problems that Celia had. She had always been close to her grandmother, so it was never a burden. But

Celia Macintosh could be stubborn and she was determined to make her own decisions, however cockeyed they might be.

This was definitely a strange turn of events, Regan mused. And if she'd invited a stranger into her life, then it was dangerous, as well. As Regan hurried back to her car, she pulled her cell phone from her pocket. But once again, there was no answer at the lodge.

This was her fault! She hadn't been to see Ceci in three weeks, leaving her vulnerable to someone who might take advantage. If her family found out, there would be hell to pay. If Ceci had already signed some of the land away, Regan would have to get the lawyers involved, and that meant a call to her father.

The sun was already down as she navigated the curves on Shore Drive. Soon the first snowflakes would fall, and in another month, winter would be looming. When the weather changed and the holidays were past, Regan and Ceci headed south to her grandmother's condo in Scottsdale.

Ceci enjoyed the warm weather and her Arizona friends, and Regan had weddings booked beginning on New Year's Eve and nearly every weekend through the end of April. On the first of May, they packed up the car and headed back to the lake.

Regan watched for the red reflectors on the trees, and when she saw them she knew the lodge was just ahead. The entrance was marked by two stone pillars, and as she steered her Subaru wagon onto the narrow asphalt drive, her headlights created eerie shadows on the surrounding trees. Ahead, the lodge was lit up from top to bottom, a habit that her grandmother had adopted her first night alone in the house.

The adjustment had been hard on Ceci. Her grandmother had been only seventy-five years old when her husband had died. She'd expected to have more time with the man she'd called her husband since age nineteen. But life didn't always work out as people dreamed, as Regan had learned all too well.

She pulled the car to a stop and turned off the ignition. Grabbing her bag, she hopped out and jogged up to the front door. Regan had her own key to the lodge, but she usually announced her arrival by ringing the bell.

"Nana?" she called as she walked inside. "Nana, it's Regan."

A few seconds later, Ceci walked in from the rear of the house. Her appearance was shocking, causing Regan to gasp out loud. Since her husband's death, her grandmother had gradually lost her flair for fashion, dressing in simple clothes in somber colors, pulling her ash-blond hair back into a tidy knot. But tonight she was wearing a flowing caftan in neon pink and tangerine orange. Her hair was styled in soft curls around her face and Regan was stunned at how young she looked.

"Nana," she whispered. "You're…stunning."

Ceci smiled, then twirled around. "This old thing? I haven't worn it in years."

"You did your hair."

"Is the style all right? I know it's not fashionable to tease one's hair anymore, but I couldn't help myself."

"You look lovely." Regan hesitated for a split second before she asked the obvious question. *Why* had Ceci gone to so much trouble? Regan drew in a slow breath. "What's the occasion?" she asked.

"I met a lovely young man at the hardware store a few weeks ago," Ceci said. "He's working on a very important project. Changing the way we think about housing. He has some papers for me to sign, so I've invited him for dinner tonight. Since you're here, you can join us. Why don't you go tidy up while I get things ready? It wouldn't hurt for you to fix your hair and put on a little lipstick."

"Is this the man you want to lease Maple Point to?"

"Walt Murphy should mind his own business. And so should you. If I choose to lease or sell Maple Point, then that's my decision—not yours."

"Do you even know who this guy is, Nana? He could be a con man, a swindler, one of those creeps that preys on elderly women with money. A wolf in sheep's clothing!"

"I haven't lost my all my senses," Ceci said. "I checked with our family attorney and Mr. Quinn seems to be exactly who he says he is. I never would have invited him to stay with me if I thought he was some sort of…ne'er-do-well."

"You invited him to stay here?" Regan asked.

"I offered to rent him the guest cottage. I could use the extra money."

"Nana, there's no reason for you to have to take in boarders. You have plenty of money. And if you're lonely you can always call me. I'll come and spend the night."

"I know, dear," she said. "But you're busy with your own life. And I need something to do with mine. Something to look forward to."

"And that's serving dinner to some stranger?"

"He's not a stranger," Ceci said. "He's a lovely man and I'm sure you'll agree when you meet him."

"Which I plan to do right now," Regan said. "When will he get here?"

"Oh, he's here already. He's upstairs," Ceci said. "I thought it would be nice if we dressed for dinner. Your grandfather and I used to do that and it always made dinner seem so much more special. He didn't have a dinner jacket, but I found an old one of your grandfather's and he said he'd make do."

Regan groaned inwardly. It was clear her grandmother was already infatuated with this man. Dinner jackets and intimate meals for two? Someone needed to put a stop to this before Ceci got hurt, and it seemed like Regan was the only one capable of doing it. "I'm just going to go upstairs and introduce myself to him," she said.

"He'll be down in a few seconds. Surely you can wait."

"No," Regan said. "I don't think this can wait." With that, she turned on her heel and started for the stairs.

When she glanced back at her grandmother, she saw a worried expression on her soft features. If this man was hoping to take advantage of her grandmother,

Regan would find out. There were so many unscru-
pulous people in the world, people capable of ruining
another person's life, people capable of stealing a person's identity. She would never allow that to happen to
her grandmother. No matter how handsome or charming the man was.

Regan climbed the log stairs to the second floor and
one by one searched the six bedrooms. She found his
things scattered on the bed in the last room and she
stepped inside to take a look.

The sound of running water filtered through the
bathroom door and she listened to it with one ear, realizing that her time to do some snooping would be
limited. Regan picked up his wallet and began to rifle
through it. She found his driver's license and pulled it
out to examine the photo. The breath froze in her throat.

"Oh, my God," she murmured. "It's him."

Though her grandmother had said he was handsome,
she'd assumed he would be a little older. The man's driver's
license revealed him to be only twenty-seven years old,
and in the picture he possessed a masculine beauty that
any woman would be grateful to have in her bed.

She found herself staring at the photograph, trying
to gauge the intent of the person behind the pale blue
eyes. There was nothing she could tell from the license,
however; nothing could be revealed beyond the fact that
his parents had made a genetically perfect male.

He had nearly five hundred dollars in his wallet,
along with a stack of credit cards. From the rest of the
contents, she discovered he had a reliable dry cleaner, a

favorite coffee shop and tickets for a Blizzard's hockey game against New York in early December.

Regan returned the wallet to where she'd found it and picked up his phone. But to her dismay, he'd turned it off. She pushed the power button and waited for the screen to light up. Certainly she'd be able to learn more from his old texts and his photo library…

JAMIE GRABBED A towel from the pile beside the shower and wrapped it around his waist. He probably shouldn't have taken the time for a shower, considering Celia was waiting with dinner downstairs, but he'd spent most of the day in the car, and the marble shower seemed like the perfect place to work out the kinks in his neck and spine.

He opened the bathroom door and stopped short when he found a woman sitting on the end of the bed, holding his phone. She glanced his way and he realized that he knew her. "It's you," he murmured, recognizing the woman from the road that morning.

She stared at him with suspicious eyes. "And it's you. Would you like to tell me what you're doing here, in my grandmother's house?"

"I think the more important question is what are you doing with my phone?"

She jumped up and dropped his phone on the bed as if it were made of fire. Her gaze slowly drifted from his damp hair to his naked chest and finally to the towel that hung low on his hips.

He chuckled softly. "I didn't expect to see you again."

She turned toward the door, obviously torn between

her desire to escape and her curiosity about the stranger standing half-naked in front of her. At the last moment, she decided to stay.

"Regan," she finally said. "I'm Regan Macintosh. I'm Celia's granddaughter. My father is Celia's middle son." She held out her hand, then realized his right hand was holding up his towel.

"It's a pleasure to meet you, Regan," he said. He made sure the towel was knotted and shook her hand. "I'm James Quinn, but everyone calls me Jamie."

She glanced down at where their fingers had become entwined, her brow furrowing as if she was confused how they'd gotten that way.

She forced a smile and Jamie waited for her to explain herself. Then, suddenly, she straightened her spine and looked him directly in the eyes.

"I think we've had enough of this," she said, waving her hand in the direction of his bare chest. "I'm sure you find it quite useful to wander about half-naked. I'm sure it makes all the ladies a little breathless and dizzy. But to me it all seems a bit desperate."

"Desperate?" Jamie chuckled softly. "How so?"

"Men like you need to use their best assets to their advantage," she explained. "It's quite apparent that you have an incredibly hot body. But I'm sure that my grandmother will be immune to such a blatant ploy."

"A blatant ploy?" he murmured. "What exactly do you think I'm doing here?"

"I assume you're here to hustle my grandmother out of her life savings. Isn't that what men like you use your bodies to do?"

A laugh burst from Jamie's throat as he realized the conclusion she'd jumped to. "You think I'm a gigolo?"

"I suppose you prefer the term con artist?" She cursed softly. "I can assure you, if you appear downstairs in just that towel, you may give her a heart attack."

Jamie shook his head, then walked to the end of the bed to pick through the clothes he'd brought along. He grabbed a pair of boxers and stepped into them, sliding them up to his waist beneath the towel. Then he pulled the towel off and draped it around his neck. "I'm here because I needed a place to stay and I didn't want to go to a motel. Your grandmother kindly offered to rent me her guest house and I accepted. Then she invited me to dinner. Nothing more, nothing less."

"Right. Don't forget about the land you're trying to swindle. You probably think that she's an easy mark, living all alone out here, with no one to watch after her. But *I'm* watching out for her," Regan said. "And you're not going to get a finger on one single dollar of her money or one single acre of her land. Do I make myself clear?"

Jamie strolled to the closet and grabbed one of the shirts he found there. Yanking it over his arms, he cursed softly. "The only thing that's clear is that you are certifiably crazy."

"I am not!" she cried.

"If you *weren't* crazy, you would politely excuse yourself, and let me get dressed on my own."

Regan opened her mouth to utter a quick reply, but her answer died on her tongue. "We're not done with this. Not by a long mile."

"I look forward to discussing this further at a mutually convenient time," Jamie said.

"There will be plenty of those," she said, "since I plan to check up on you for as long as you're here."

"Fine!" he said.

"Fine!" she shot back. "I'll see you downstairs."

Jamie watched her storm out of the room, his gaze taking in a delicious view of her backside. This was an interesting development, he mused. In truth, he was glad to have Regan around. If any of the other family members objected, Regan could provide proof that he was dealing fairly with Celia and that he had no intentions of cheating her out of anything.

Though Regan was dead wrong about his intentions, she was right about one thing. Her grandmother did seem to be excited at the prospect of company. And maybe he did use that to his advantage to get a perfect room in a perfect house on a perfect piece of property. But it was an innocent friendship, and he was expert enough at short-term relationships to make sure no one got hurt.

He finished buttoning the shirt, which luckily fit fairly well, then walked over to the mirror and raked his fingers through his still-damp hair.

Now his interest in Regan Macintosh, on the other hand... He couldn't say his intentions would remain innocent where she was concerned.

He picked up the dinner jacket Celia had given him and shrugged into it, then headed downstairs, preparing himself for a lively evening with two beautiful women.

When he entered the kitchen, Celia turned and

clapped her hands. "Don't you look debonair," she said, her eyes bright. She reached up and adjusted the collar of his shirt. "I guessed right that you'd be about the same size as Kenneth."

Regan cleared her throat and Celia glanced over her shoulder at her granddaughter. "Didn't you two introduce yourselves?" she asked, glancing between him and Regan.

Jamie smiled and shrugged, and he watched Regan bristle at the thought of repeating what had happened upstairs.

"I know who he is, Nana. You told me his name."

"But there are common courtesies that we observe in this house. Regan, darling, this is Mr. James Quinn. He'd like us to call him Jamie. Jamie, this is my favorite granddaughter, Regan Macintosh."

Jamie reached out and took her fingertips into the palm of his hand. He ignored the rush of heat that raced through his body. It was a natural reaction, he mused. It had been a while since he had been with a woman, and Regan had just seen him half-naked. He drew her hand to his lips and placed a kiss just below her wrist. "It's a pleasure to meet you," he murmured.

She watched him intently, her expression one of barely concealed indifference. God, she was a challenge. He felt like a schoolboy, teasing the prettiest girl in class just to get a rise from her.

"Look how good he is at that, Nana," Regan said. "So smooth. No one does that anymore." She snatched her hand away. "No one."

"Regan! Don't be rude." Ceci held out her own hand and Jamie dutifully kissed it.

"I'm not being rude. Is it rude to ask Mr. Quinn what his true intentions are here? He seems to have waltzed in and taken over a spot at the table, wearing my grandfather's dinner jacket. And you seem…bewitched!"

Jamie cleared his throat, more as a warning than an intention to talk. Regan glanced over at her grandmother and noticed the two bright spots of embarrassment on her cheeks. "I'm sorry. I didn't mean that."

"Of course you did, darling. I can't blame you. And I won't lie. I have been lonely, and it's been nice for an attractive man to wander into my life and provide a bit of excitement."

"Nana, you don't have to—"

"Having Mr. Quinn here has been a refreshing change of pace. But he is my guest and I will decide if and when he leaves." She clapped her hands together and forced a smile. "Now that we've cleared that up, I do believe dinner is ready."

DINNER WAS A lively affair, reminding Regan of the time before her grandfather had died. She hadn't seen her grandmother smile so much in years, and it made Regan happy that sparkling conversation with a handsome man was all it took to bring the light back into Ceci's eyes.

Of course, Jamie did his part, with clever compliments, silly stories and endless charm. And it wasn't just her grandmother who suffered the effects. He turned his considerable charm in Regan's direction, as well.

But she could sense that his intentions weren't so innocent with her. He seemed to take delight in irritating her, and she seemed to be unable to control her temper around him. They were waging a silent battle, jockeying for position, trying to read the other's next move. And though he'd provided a reasonable character reference for himself, she still found herself wary and on edge.

Maybe it was the fact that he could kiss her wrist and her whole body seemed to go weak. Or he could smile at her and her heart felt as if it were about to leap out of her chest. She couldn't seem to control her reactions to him, and though fascinating, it was also dangerous.

If she couldn't control herself, how could she possibly control him? Control was an absolute requirement when it came to her relationships with men. It was the only way to protect herself, the only way to maintain a safe distance.

Regan listened distractedly as he talked about his job and explained the project he was working on and the cottage he planned to build. Habikit. She remembered reading something about his company in a recent issue of the newspaper, but she didn't remember seeing a picture of him. She would've remembered that.

By the time dinner was over and dessert had been served, they'd managed to finish off two bottles of expensive red wine. Her grandmother had nursed the same glass throughout the entire evening, so Regan realized that she and Jamie must have drunk the rest.

She didn't feel intoxicated, but she did feel pleasantly relaxed. And though her tongue occasionally got tangled, Regan wrote that off to being in the company of a handsome man.

"Would anybody like coffee?" Celia asked.

Jamie pushed back from the table and stood up. "Why don't you ladies relax and I'll make the coffee and clean up the dishes."

"No, no, no," Celia said. "You're my guest and I won't have you doing chores."

"Actually, I wouldn't mind helping out around the house," Jamie said. "I'm sure there are plenty of things that might appreciate a man's touch."

Regan was in the middle of taking a sip of wine when he made his last statement, and she began to cough at his blatant offer of sexual favors.

"Are you all right, darling?" Celia asked. Regan waved her hand in front of her face, slowly realizing that the meaning she took from his words wasn't what he'd intended.

"I'm sorry. I just drank that a little too fast. Let me help with the coffee."

She and Jamie gathered the dirty plates and silver and headed back to the kitchen.

Jamie stood at the sink and began to rinse the dishes while Regan finished clearing, then she took her place on the other side of him and loaded the dishes into the dishwasher.

"I should probably apologize," Jamie said. "You probably assumed that offer to help around the house had sexual overtones."

"Really?" Regan said. "No, I didn't notice."

Jamie chuckled. "Oh, yes you did. You nearly choked on your wine."

Regan surrendered a smile. "All right, maybe I did.

But you have to admit, your words could be taken both ways."

"You, my dear, have a dirty mind. And the sooner you realize I'm a respectable man, the easier it will be for us to get along with each other."

"Why would I want to get along with you?" Regan asked.

"Because I'm endlessly fascinating and I tell a good story."

"And not because you have an overinflated ego and narcissistic personality disorder?"

"I think if you gave me a chance," Jamie said, "you'd like me."

"I'm sure you've had a lot of women who have liked you," she said, "only to get their hearts broken."

He chuckled softly. "Yeah, you'd think. But that's not the way it's worked out. I'm the one who usually gets his heart broken."

The coffee was finished and Regan set it on a tray along with a trio of cups and saucers, as well as cream and sugar. The moment her grandmother saw the tray, Celia shook her head. "I can't have any coffee now," she said. "I'll never fall asleep if I do." She slowly got to her feet. "You'll stay here tonight," she said to Jamie. "Take the bedroom you got dressed in." She turned to Regan. "And you'll be nice. I'll see you both in the morning. Good night."

Jamie joined her at the table and they both watched as Celia walked out of the room, leaving the two of them alone together.

Regan reached out and poured herself a cup of coffee.

She added a good measure of sugar, then took a long sip. Though it tasted good, coffee did little to counteract the wine she'd drunk.

He stared at her from the other side of the table. Regan knew if she looked at him, just simply met his gaze, she'd want him to crawl over the table and kiss her. And she wasn't ready for that.

"I—I could use some fresh air," she murmured. "I'll just be a moment."

Regan walked through the great room to the tall wall of windows that overlooked the water. She grabbed a red knit shawl from a hook near the door and wrapped it around her head, then walked out into the chilly night air.

A shiver skittered down her spine, but she wasn't sure it was because of the cold or due to being in such close proximity to Jamie. Her footsteps echoed softly on the wood deck and when she reached the railing, Regan spread her hands out on the rough wood and drew a deep breath. The fresh air immediately cleared her head.

Regan heard the door open behind her and she held her breath, counting his steps as he approached. She shivered again, this time her teeth chattering with the cold.

"What is this thing you're wearing?" he asked, fingering the fabric of the cape. "You look like Little Red Riding Hood."

"It's vintage," she said.

"And that makes it stylish?"

"Of course," Regan teased. "And I like the color. Red is one of my favorites." Her teeth chattered again and she moved away from him. A moment later she felt the warmth of his jacket surrounding her. He'd pulled his jacket open and he stood behind her, his arms wrapped around her chest, her back pressed against his warm body.

"Better?"

It was better. But it was also more frightening. And more exhilarating. And more confusing. And yet it seemed perfectly natural. "I should probably get to bed, too," Regan said. "It's been a while since I've had so much wine and I can't afford to fall asleep at work tomorrow."

He slowly turned her around in his arms until she faced him. His lips were dangerously close to hers, so close she could feel the warmth of his breath on her cheek.

"I know you still don't trust me, but you're attracted to me. I'm attracted to you, too. I want to kiss you," he whispered. "Why don't we just see where this goes?"

"I think that might be a mistake," she replied.

Her answer seemed to take him by surprise. "Then I guess we'll leave it for another time," he said. "Good night, Regan." With that he turned and walked off the deck.

Regan released a tightly held breath and it clouded in the cold air in front of her face. Her heart slammed in her chest and she realized how close she'd come to surrender. He was right; she was attracted to him. She had wanted to kiss him. She'd been thinking about it all night. But in the end common sense won out.

Regan slowly smiled. She *was* strong enough. She

could control her emotions when he touched her. Though he still was dangerous, he wasn't a Superman. He was just an ordinary guy. And if she could call the shots, maybe she could let something happen between them.

Maybe he'd ask again tomorrow. Maybe then she'd say yes.

3

JAMIE LOCKED HIS hands behind his head and stared up at the ceiling of the spacious bedroom. Somewhere deep inside the house he heard three chimes announce that it was now three o'clock. He tried to fall asleep, but his thoughts kept returning to the events of the day and the time he'd spent with Regan.

It was hard to comprehend that she was just a few feet away from him, curled up in her own bed and perhaps unaffected by their meeting. Jamie couldn't say the same for himself.

He threw the covers aside and stood up, then wandered over to the empty hearth.

Outside the wind had picked up and the temperature had dropped even lower. He thought of the construction ahead of him. Building in the cold wasn't impossible, but it wouldn't be as comfortable. The sooner he got started the better. Now that he had the permits, his next step was to finalize the lease and survey the site. He'd need a day or two to clear the trees that had to come down and then he'd be ready to start building.

Jamie closed his eyes and counted through the days. He could start the footings in about a week and then start construction. That still gave him a few days' wiggle room in case of bad weather and build problems. His hard deadline was the last day of October.

On November 1, a group of investors were coming from Los Angeles to visit the factory and the cottage model. If they invested, Jamie would get back the money he'd loaned the company. He'd no longer be risking his own future. And the company that meant so much to him would have a much more stable future.

Regan was a complication. She was smart and beautiful and the kind of challenge he enjoyed. And she was a huge distraction. A beautiful distraction with sparkling green eyes and whiskey-colored hair and a spirit that tempted him.

Groaning softly, Jamie turned away from the hearth and walked back to the bed. His stomach growled and the sound immediately reminded him of his childhood, so many empty stomachs and missed meals. Nights spent sleeping in a park or in the backseat of an abandoned car rather than the elegant bedroom of the lakeside lodge.

A soft knock sounded on the door and Jamie looked up. He grabbed his robe from the end of the bed and shrugged into it, holding it closed in front. Then he crossed the room and opened the door. Regan stood outside in the hall, dressed entirely in flannel.

"You're still awake," she said. "Is there anything I can get you?"

"Sure. Yeah. I guess I could use something to eat. Or drink."

"I was headed to the kitchen myself."

He slipped out into the hallway and followed her down the wide steps to the lower floor. They walked directly to the kitchen, and when they got there Regan opened the freezer drawer.

"My grandmother's crazy for ice cream, so she usually has six or seven flavors to choose from. Do you like ice cream?"

"Who doesn't?" Jamie said, choosing the cherry flavor. "I used to dream about it as a kid."

"I wanted to apologize for earlier," she said, taking out a carton for herself. "For assuming you were here to take advantage of my grandmother. I looked you up on the internet and your company is real and it's doing good things."

"No, you had every right to be suspicious. These days, you never know who to trust. I would've done the same thing with my own grandmother."

"Do you see her often?"

"My brothers and I have Sunday dinner with her at her house once a month," he said. "And I stop by to mow the lawn or shovel snow occasionally."

"I don't know what I would've done without my grandmother," Regan said. "She helped me through some tough times."

"Mine, too," Jamie said. "We lived with her after my parents split up."

It was his customary way to explain his childhood, and though it was a lie, it usually didn't elicit more questions. His parents really hadn't split up. His father had been killed trying to rob a gas station. And his mother, caught up in a drug addiction, had been in and out of jail.

"How old were you when they divorced?"

"They never divorced. They just…well, they just went their separate ways. We—my brothers and I—were left to raise ourselves."

"You don't need to tell me. It's none of my business."

No one ever wanted to hear about an unhappy childhood. That's why Jamie never revealed the whole truth.

She gave them each a spoon and started eating out of the carton. He took a bite of the ice cream and smiled. "It's not a problem," he said. "They were better off apart. And my brothers and I got along just fine."

"Do you see much of your parents?"

Jamie shook his head. "No. I guess you could say we're estranged. But it's for the best."

Regan let out a long sigh, avoiding his gaze. "I'm sorry."

That was the reaction he hated the most. Pity. He never felt sorry for himself, and he didn't expect others to, either. "It's all in the past. I don't think about it a lot."

"Tell me more about the project you're working on," Regan asked.

"I'm really excited about all the applications the homes will have. They're packed into modules that are easy to ship. So you can load them on a truck and take them to a hurricane zone or a flood zone. Wherever temporary housing is needed. They can also be used for portable classrooms and other temporary space. Think about what our company could have done in Haiti if we'd been up and running."

He put the cherry ice cream back in line with the others and chose a new flavor, toffee caramel. "We've got some investors interested in giving us a nice chunk of money, but they want to see the modules built out. That's why we're building this cottage model on Pickett Lake. Once we have the investment secure, we can ramp up production and start to take orders. And I'll start traveling around the country promoting the homeless project. We've had a good response so far and I hope the concept won't be too hard to sell, especially since a lot of it is made of recycled materials. Green is a very big selling point these days."

Regan stared at him, shaking her head.

"What? I know, once I get talking about it, I can't seem to stop. My partners tell me I have to streamline my sales pitch, but I always want to put it all in there. And I didn't even mention the applications this has for the elderly."

"No, it was a very good pitch. And I'm convinced that you aren't some kind of con man who preys on elderly women. I was wrong. I'm sorry for being so suspicious."

"I forgive you," Jamie teased, pleased that she'd finally seen the light. "People make that mistake all the time." He took another bite of his ice cream. "Now it's your turn. Your grandmother tells me you're a photographer. Besides photographs of runaway foxes, what do you shoot?"

"Weddings, babies," Regan said. "Happy occasions. I have a small studio in town, but almost all my photos are taken on-site. I work here during the summer and then go south with Ceci to Arizona for the winter."

"Would you show me your photos?" he said.

"I have a really nice one of a guy who scared away those foxes. You might recognize him."

Chuckling, Jamie put the top back on the carton and then got up and circled the granite-covered island. He handed her the carton. "Thank you. I needed that."

"Me, too," she replied, gathering up the cartons and returning them to the freezer.

They walked together toward the stairs. Regan faced him, her hand resting on the newel post. "I am attracted to you." A wicked smile curled the corners of her mouth. "But I'm still not sure it's a good idea to explore that."

"Maybe you should give it a try and see what happens."

Regan seemed surprised by his challenge. "Maybe I should," she said with a shrug. "Some other time, perhaps."

She started up the stairs, but Jamie grabbed her and pulled her back into his arms.

His lips met hers in a sweet, urgent kiss filled with breathless longing and simmering desire. His hands skimmed the length of her arms, then cupped her face, drawing her more deeply into the kiss.

She tasted like sweet chocolate with just a hint of caramel. Jamie smiled, his lips drifting lower, to her neck and then her shoulder. She leaned against him, and he held her waist tight as he pulled her down on top of him as he sank onto the carpeted stairs.

She braced her hands on either side of his head as their hips met. His hard shaft pressed against the soft flesh of her belly. Every time she shifted above him, wild sensations raced through his body.

He furrowed his hands in her hair, dragging her lips across his again. His tongue probed deeper, desperate for more. He felt his control teeter on the edge and he drew back, staring up into her green eyes.

She reached down and touched his damp lips with her fingertips. Jamie wanted to pull her back into the kiss, but she pushed off of him and sat on the steps beside him.

"I should go back to bed. I have a busy day tomorrow."

Jamie took her hand and drew it to his lips. "Did I go too far?"

She shook her head. "No! Oh, no, it was nice." She studied her fingertips. "Lovely…perfect," she said, her hair tumbling around her face in careless waves.

She was so beautiful that just looking at her made him ache inside. He wanted to take her into his arms and kiss her again. Better yet, he wanted to scoop her up and carry her to his bedroom, where he could take his time with her.

But he didn't want to rush things. Until she trusted him completely, he'd let her call the shots. Jamie pushed to his feet, then held out his hand and helped her up. "I'll walk you to your door," he said.

They climbed the log stairs together, and when they reached Regan's bedroom door, Jamie cupped her face in his hands and gave her one last kiss. "Good night, Regan. I hope I see you again tomorrow."

"Good night," she said, reaching back to open the door. She slipped inside and the latch clicked behind her.

THE NEXT MORNING, Regan examined her reflection in the bathroom mirror, pressing her fingertips to her slightly swollen lips. She smiled to herself, recalling their intense encounter on the stairs, the long, delicious kisses. The deep, sweet ache of need she'd felt. And the anticipation that seemed to follow even his most innocent of caresses.

After making her escape, Regan had spent most of the night wide-awake, thinking of him just a few feet away. She'd wondered what was going through his head. Was he tempted to cross that small distance, throw caution to the wind and see if she'd open the door to him? Or was it her turn to be the aggressor? Was he waiting for her to make the next move? She had been the one to put the brakes on last night, after all.

She wanted answers. Regan was the kind of woman who had to know exactly where she stood at all times. There would be no surprises with Jamie. If she allowed him into her life, she would be the one to usher him out.

Yet all her determination to keep control seemed to melt away the moment he touched her. One minute, she knew exactly what she was doing, and the next, she was ready to jump in with no idea how far she'd fall.

She couldn't blame him for being confused by her actions. He might think she was playing some silly game, and Regan hated games. She ought to explain exactly what she wanted from him. He'd admire her honesty, and she'd be able to set the rules.

Regan glanced at her watch. It was nearly nine o'clock. She had a consult with a wedding planner at ten, a bride who wanted to order some special prints coming in at eleven. If Jamie was downstairs, she'd have just enough time to explain her behavior the previous night. Waiting until dinner would be excruciating.

She shoved her makeup bag in her purse and checked her appearance one last time. She always left a few outfits at her grandmother's in case she spent the night, and last time she'd left one of her favorite dresses. She'd put it on today to give her an extra boost of confidence. "All right," she murmured. "You've done all you can." One look would be enough for her to know exactly how Jamie felt about last night.

When Regan got downstairs, she was surprised to find her grandmother sitting alone at the kitchen island. Usually Ceci preferred to sleep until nine or ten, so it was unusual for Regan to see her before she left for the day. "Hello, there," she said, walking over to kiss her grandmother's cheek. "You're up early"

"I waste far too much time lying in bed," her grandmother replied.

"Is your houseguest sleeping late?"

"Oh, no, darling. He's already up and gone. I made breakfast for him at six-thirty and he was out of the house by sunrise."

Regan tried to appear indifferent to the news, but

she couldn't help but be disappointed that she'd missed him. Or that her grandmother had gotten to spend time with him that morning and she hadn't. She cursed inwardly. This was ridiculous! She felt like a schoolgirl with a crush on her best friend's guy. "Well, he seems to be a hard worker."

Her grandmother smiled coyly. "Yes, he does, doesn't he?"

Regan pushed away from the counter and went to the coffeemaker. She grabbed a mug, filled it and sat down across from her grandmother. "Ceci, are you sure you should invest so much in a man you don't know?"

"Invest? I'm not sure what you mean."

Regan thought for a moment before she spoke. She'd have to handle this very delicately. If her grandmother had formed an attachment to the man, then she couldn't discount that easily. Simply because there was a nearly fifty-year age difference between the two of them didn't mean they couldn't be good friends, and Regan didn't want to deny her grandmother a new friend. "You're making him breakfast, and fancy dinners, and shifting your whole life so it revolves around him. Sooner or later he's going to leave and then what will you have?"

Her grandmother took a long sip of her coffee as she considered her answer. "I suppose I'll have what I always have," she said. "My memories."

Regan felt a surge of guilt at her grandmother's lonely words. "I just don't want to see you get hurt."

Ceci reached out and covered Regan's hand with hers, giving it a pat. "I can take care of myself," she murmured. "I'm not afraid of getting hurt. It's just good to feel something at all. I went to bed last night excited for the next day."

Regan gave her grandmother's hand a squeeze. "I just want you to be happy," she said. "And I know it's been difficult for you since Grandfather died."

"I can't imagine what he'd think," Ceci said. "I know he would like Jamie. What's not to like? But he might think I'm being silly for trying to be friends with someone so much younger." She paused, then drew a deep breath. "And maybe I am being silly. But I feel young again. And maybe it's time I got back into the world."

"I don't want this to become too much for you," Regan said.

"It won't be, I promise. But there is one thing you could help me with."

"Anything," Regan said.

"I want you to come shopping with me. All my clothes seem so out-of-date. I want something fun. And I want to get my hair done. Something that doesn't take a can of hair spray to keep in place."

Regan studied her grandmother for a long moment. "You're not afraid, are you?"

"Why should I be afraid? Everyone should live their fullest life. Chances don't always come in a package we might recognize, but that doesn't mean we shouldn't enjoy them when they come." She paused. "There have been a lot of things that have surprised me as I've grown older. But I think the most frustrating thing is that, while my outward appearance has aged, I still feel like a young woman inside. Life might have worn out my body, but not my spirit."

"Isn't that a good thing?" Regan asked.

"I'm not sure. I want more from the rest of my life, not less. I don't want to waste a minute. But that's not how I'm supposed to behave. I'm supposed to slow down, but I don't want to slow down."

"Nana, you can live your life however you want. No one is going to judge you."

"Yes, they will," Ceci said. "You have. Right now, you're thinking I'm a little bit crazy."

Regan recognized the truth in her words. "I'm sorry. I might have, at first. But I don't anymore. I suppose I could learn a few things from you."

Ceci stood and took her coffee mug to the sink. "You've let that awful wedding stop you from finding romance. I will never forgive that man for what he did to you."

Regan shook her head. "Maybe we should forgive him. I suppose I should be happy that I didn't marry him."

Ceci turned and faced her, leaning back against the edge of the counter. "Maybe, but tell me that you haven't completely given up on love," she said.

Regan had never lied to her grandmother and she didn't want to start now. "I haven't given up on passion. I'm just not sure about love. That's so much more complicated. To fall in love you have to surrender yourself. You know me. I need to be in control."

"But I'd hate to see you miss out."

Regan sighed. "Someday maybe I'll figure it all out like you have," she teased. She rounded the kitchen island and put her mug in the sink. "I have an idea. Why don't I finish up work early today and we'll drive into the city and shop. We can get your hair styled and we can get manis and pedis. It will be the perfect girls' day out."

"I'll have to be home by three," Ceci said. "I have a meeting with Jamie and the lawyers to sign papers on the property."

"Ceci, we need to talk about this deal you're making. I know you admire his company's goals—I do, too. But Maple Point is a valuable piece of property. Just handing it to him may not be a good thing to do. Instead of giving him Maple Point, why don't you lease him a bit of shoreline on the other side of the lodge?"

"That's just rock and scrub brush," Ceci said. "It's not nearly as pretty as Maple Point."

"Well, I think we should consider offering that to him instead. I'm sure he'd be happy to have any piece of shoreline, as long as you were charging a decent price."

She had to admit that she was as anxious to see Jamie as her grandmother was. And she couldn't say yet that that she had complete control over her attraction to the man. But when it came to the land, she knew exactly where she stood. Jamie Quinn was not going to get Maple Point. Not as long as she was here to stop him.

"Get your purse, your credit cards and a pair of comfy shoes," Regan said. "We have work to do."

"I feel like Cinderella," Ceci said, her eyes bright with excitement.

"And I'm your fairy granddaughter," Regan teased.

Perhaps she shouldn't encourage her grandmother. Who knew where this new zest for life would lead Ceci?

But she was happy and optimistic, no longer mourning the past but looking toward the future. The company of a younger man seemed to have done wonders for her attitude toward life.

But what would a full-fledged sexual fixation do to Regan? She'd never know unless she tried. The lure of a purely physical relationship with a man like Jamie was hard to resist. And if she waited around for conditions to be absolutely perfect, it might never happen.

He'd said he needed to have the project completed in just a few weeks, which meant she didn't have long. If she dragged her feet, she might miss out on something truly amazing. And as long as he agreed to a short-term affair, they could share a bed that very night.

Chances were he'd agree that a no-strings relationship was for the best. Three weeks was perfect timing—not too long, not too short. No time for emotions to become involved.

And of course, no mixing business with pleasure. She was still adamant that Jamie shouldn't build on the point. If she couldn't convince him to take the other piece of land, there was every chance that he'd walk out of her life for good.

JAMIE OPENED THE front door of the lodge and ushered in the two attorneys, one man representing Jamie's company and the other appearing for Celia. They were here to finalize the leasing agreement for Celia's pretty little point.

Regan's grandmother had already given her blessing to the deal, so they were down to negotiating a price and a lease term that Jamie, his partners and Celia would agree to. He'd already sold Celia on the concept, so Jamie didn't expect any serious roadblocks.

As he passed through the house, the lawyers following him, he noticed Celia sitting at the computer in the library. "Just head on through there," he said to the two men, pointing to the great room. "I'll be with you in a second."

Jamie knocked softly on the library door and Celia spun around to face him, her reading glasses perched on the end of her nose. "Hello," she said.

"Sorry to interrupt."

Her eyes were bright with excitement. "I used to be afraid of this thing, but it's really quite simple."

"The computer?"

"Facebook. Do you know Facebook? It's the most amazing thing. I can keep track of all my grandchildren. And Twitter? Regan wrote out a whole list for me."

"They're all fun, but we have our meeting with the lawyers. They're here."

She waved her hand distractedly. "I had a talk with Regan this afternoon and she made some interesting points about our deal. I'm going to let her handle everything from here on out. She's much better at negotiations than I could ever be." She held up a shiny new cell phone. "Besides, I have to figure out how to use this next. I can talk to my grandchildren with this thing and Regan says I can even see their faces while I'm doing it. Amazing, don't you think?"

She turned back to her computer and Jamie cursed inwardly. What the hell was going on? He thought the deal had been made. He had the permits and was ready to start building next week. And now Regan had distracted her grandmother with some shiny new toys while she set herself up as the deal maker?

They had a verbal agreement. And Ceci had signed a preliminary agreement, as well. By law, Regan was going to have a hard time fighting the terms. He walked to the rear of the lodge. Regan was waiting there with the lawyers. She smiled at him and pointed to a chair at the table.

"Let's get down to business," she said. "Gentlemen, I'm Regan Macintosh. Celia's granddaughter. And from now on, you'll be dealing with me."

They spent the next half hour in a frustrating back-and-forth, Jamie offering terms and Regan flatly turning him down each time. She wasn't even attempting to negotiate, and he couldn't tell whether he just hadn't reached her price yet or whether she was determined to scuttle the deal no matter what he offered.

She insisted that Maple Point was off the table, to be replaced by a piece of shoreline on the opposite side of the lodge. His permits would still be good and he could still complete the project on time. But he hadn't even seen that piece of land. He had no idea how accessible it would be or whether it would make the best setting for his showroom.

"Gentlemen, I think we're wasting your time here. It's clear that we're a lot further apart than I thought. So I suggest that Miss Macintosh and I take a few days to try and work out our differences and we'll call you back in when we do."

Jamie walked the attorneys to the front door, doing his best to hide his frustration. Then he hunted for Regan. He found her in the kitchen, pouring herself a glass of lemonade.

"Thank you *so* much for that," Jamie said. "It's not as if I don't worry about finances twenty-four hours a day as it is. And now I've paid our attorney to drive an hour each way and bill me for at least three hours of wasted time. You may have a vault filled with gold and jewels, but I don't. I'm on a budget."

He cursed softly as he paced the length of the kitchen. "Have I wasted my time, as well? Celia and I had a verbal agreement. The offers I made were fair. But I get the sense this is about something else."

He stopped in front of her, clenching his fists. Her gaze met his and he shook his head. "This is some kind of game with you, isn't it?"

"No," she said. "I know exactly what my motives are. I'm just not sure they match yours. And until I am, I'm not going to agree to your terms."

Jamie turned and walked over to the doors leading out to the deck. He yanked one of them open and stepped outside. When he reached the railing, he braced his hands on the cold iron and drew in a deep breath.

If she wasn't going to negotiate, he could try going around her to Ceci. But was he prepared to pit Celia against her granddaughter? Was he willing to enforce the verbal agreement that a seventy-five-year-old woman had made on a whim? Just how desperate was he? But if not, he'd have to find someplace else to build, and there was no way he could do that and still make his time line.

He heard the door open behind him and closed his eyes. Why did there have to be this business between them? Life would have been so much easier if it could have been pure pleasure. Then kissing her wouldn't seem like a life or death decision.

She joined him at the railing. "After my grandfather died, my grandmother just fell apart. She was strong through the funeral and in front of everyone while they were here. But then people went home and got on with their lives, and she was all alone for the first time in her life. So I stayed with her. And after a while, it became my responsibility to look after her. I wasn't married, I had a flexible schedule, I liked Pickett Lake."

"And you love your grandmother," he added.

"I do. And I love this lodge and this land. One night, about a year ago, we watched some home movies and there was some video of all of the grandchildren camping at Maple Point. Ceci said she was grateful that I had been there for her when she needed me, and that she was going to leave me Maple Point in her will. Or she'd give it to me on my wedding day, whichever came first."

"Why didn't you say something earlier?" Jamie asked.

Regan smiled and shook her head. "I didn't want to believe that my grandmother had given up on me."

"Given up?"

"That she thought I'd never find someone to love."

"Maybe she just forgot she made you that promise. She's seventy-five years old."

"She forgets a lot of things," Regan said. "And it

frightens her when she does. And this is something pretty big to forget."

"So you don't want to ask her because it might upset her," Jamie said. "You know I can't lease the land if it's part of a bequest. Your grandmother would have to change her will."

"My grandfather used to own nearly the whole western shore of this lake. Over the years the land has been sold off, and now all that our family owns is this property. After my grandmother dies, the rest of the family will sell the lodge. No one is going to want it. No one can afford to buy it. But I could have Maple Point. There would still be a spot on this lake where I could remember summers with my grandparents. Do you understand?"

Jamie drew a deep breath. "I want to."

"But it's all about the deal for you?"

"No," he said. "I just never… My family never had anything worth passing down. My grandmother has a few photo albums. And some costume jewelry. And her Sunday china." Jamie chuckled, shaking his head. "Money changes so many things."

"I suspect that your grandmother's Sunday china is as dear to her as Maple Point is to me," Regan said.

"You're probably right." He turned and faced her. "I've invested every last penny I have in this business. I need to get this model built by November 1, when we have our first investors meeting scheduled. That's less than a month away. If I need to move on, you have to tell me right now and I'll be on my way."

"Take the other piece of property. I promise you that

it's not quite as picturesque as the point, but it will serve your purposes," Regan said. "And once the business is out of the way, we can move on to pleasure."

"Pleasure? What exactly are you saying?"

"I'm saying you were right. That we should see where this leads. You're only here for a couple of weeks. I'm not looking for anything complicated. So why not enjoy ourselves?"

"You make it sound so easy."

"Isn't it?"

"No, I think this is going to be complicated as hell."

She pushed away from the rail to return to the warmth of the house. But he caught her hand and pulled her into his embrace.

"But that doesn't mean I don't want in."

He pressed her body into his, his hand firm on the small of her back. An instant later, his lips met hers in a long, desperate kiss. He'd been thinking about this moment since the last time he'd kissed her, wondering what might throw them back together, how she'd react to his mouth on hers, the taste of his tongue.

All the anger and frustration seemed to disappear in that moment and all Jamie could do was surrender to his impulses. He ran his tongue along the crease of her lips, inviting her to open beneath him. And when she did, Regan moaned softly.

But a few seconds later, she pulled back and shook her head. "Business first, then pleasure. You won't convince me to change my mind about the point by kissing me," she murmured breathlessly.

"That's not what I was doing," he said.

"Good. Because it wouldn't work, anyway."

Jamie watched her go back inside, then let out a tightly held breath. He had what he needed—a piece of land for his project. He ought to be happy and starting to plan the build. Instead, his mind was full of Regan. Which was exactly why she was dangerous.

Jamie wouldn't get any sleep if she was close by. He'd drive back to the city and stay at Tristan's place, then get the lease offer squared away in the morning.

Maybe it was for the best to put some distance between them. Then once he had his lease, he'd get to work on the build.

But he had no illusions that he'd be able to stay away indefinitely. They would be together. Not tonight, but one night. Soon.

4

REGAN GLANCED UP at the clock on the wall of her studio. Only five minutes had passed since the last time she'd looked and she scolded herself inwardly for her impatience. Jamie had called a few hours ago and said that he was on his way back to the lake.

They'd spent just one night apart and already she was anxious to see him again. She groaned softly and buried her face in her hands. This was crazy! They'd known each other for four short days and she'd already managed to become entirely infatuated with him.

Her cell phone rang and she snatched it up, hoping to find Jamie's name on the caller ID. But instead she saw her mother's name. Reluctantly, she pressed the button and held it up to her ear. "Hi, Mom."

"Hello, dear, how are you?" Helen Macintosh had always been a helicopter mom, hovering over her three daughters, making sure they never made a wrong decision or a faulty move. She'd been trying to pull the strings in their lives for years.

But lately, Regan had been snipping away at the strings, much to her mother's chagrin. It was Helen's dearest wish to see her youngest daughter happily married, and she was determined to prove that her enthusiastic support of Regan's former fiancé was just a lapse in judgment.

"I hadn't heard from you in a while. I thought I'd call and check in."

There wasn't a trace of tension in her mother's voice. She obviously hadn't heard about Celia's plan to lease Maple Point.

"I'm fine," Regan replied. It wasn't exactly the truth. She felt confused, anxious, depressed, exhilarated and exhausted. But relating her dilemma to her mother would result in an eight-hour phone conversation. "Everything is great. I had a wedding last weekend and I was just going over the photos. They want to use one of them for the cover of *Country Bride*."

"Are they going to pay you?"

"Yes, Mother, they are. And it will also be great publicity. A photo credit like that could get me another two or three jobs a year." She paused. "You know, the magazine editors suggested that I could get a lot more jobs if I worked on the East Coast during the summer instead of Minnesota. I've turned down a few opportunities out there because I didn't want to spend all my time traveling."

"Darling, once you get married and have a family, you won't be able to keep working like this. Why bother making changes now?"

"Because my career is important to me," Regan said. "But I could never leave Ceci."

"I worry about you, dear. How are you ever going to meet a man if you spend every weekend working and all your free time with your grandmother?"

"I meet plenty of men, Mother. I'm just not interested in dating. I'm too busy."

"I'd just like to see you settled, like your sisters." She paused. "I ran into Jake's mother last week. He's single again. Julia said he's never quite gotten over you. She said he had a girlfriend that they didn't approve of. Some lingerie model from Chicago."

"He's the one who forgot to hang around for our wedding ceremony!" Regan said, her temper flaring. "I don't want to talk about Jake."

The bell above the door jingled. "I have to go. Someone just walked in. I'll talk to you soon." Regan cursed softly, shaking her head. She'd been tempted to tell her mother about meeting Jamie, but it would only have spurred a never-ending barrage of questions from Helen.

She tossed her phone onto her worktable and walked around the corner to the spacious room that served as her gallery. Regan smiled when she saw Jamie standing near the door. "You're back."

"I am." He glanced around, taking in the array of photos mounted on the walls. Regan had always been proud of her work, but now she wished her subject matter was more serious. Babies and brides and the occasional dog. Not the kind of photos that would interest a man like Jamie Quinn.

"So this is what you do with your time," he murmured as he strolled around the perimeter of the gallery.

"It pays the bills," she replied.

Jamie stopped in front of a large print—a photo of a bride and groom standing alone at the end of a long dock. The sun was setting and the sky was ablaze with color. It was one of Regan's "almost perfect" shots. The subjects were looking out at the lake instead of each other. She should have changed the pose, but she been captivated by the light.

"This is beautiful," Jamie said. "It's what I imagine marriage should be like. Two people facing life together." He glanced over at her. "But I have no idea if that's right. When it comes to marriage, I have no reference points."

"No one really knows. I mean, you think you do, but you never really understand what's going on in the other person's head. It's a leap of faith, that's all. Just a giant leap of faith."

"Do I detect a hint of the cynic in you?"

He smiled at her and Regan felt her cheeks warm with a blush. She shrugged. "A cynical wedding photographer? Not very good for business." She turned back to the photo. "As for these two, they divorced two years after the wedding. And all my photos are now a bitter reminder of how they fooled themselves into believing love was real."

Jamie's eyes locked with hers for a long moment and Regan held her breath. Did he believe everything she'd said to him yesterday? That she didn't want to play some game, all she wanted was to explore the passion between them? She wanted to assure him that she knew the difference between desire and love. She drew a deep breath and plunged forward. "I suppose by looking at all these photos, you must think I'm some kind of silly romantic. But I'm not."

He ran his hands down her arms, then slipped his palms around her waist. "You aren't?"

Regan shook her head. "I realize this thing between us is only temporary. That's the way I want it. We have three weeks. We could dance around each other and pretend that there's no attraction, but I think we should just be honest. I want you. You want me. It's simple and physical. No strings attached." There. She'd asked for what she wanted and made her terms clear. "Take it or leave it."

"This is far from simple," he said, drawing her closer. "But I'll agree to your terms."

Her hips brushed against his and his hand drifted down to rest on her waist, holding her tight. "I think you might want to kiss me," she said, her gaze fixed on his mouth.

His lips curled into a playful smile. "I'm pretty sure you're the one who wants to kiss me."

"Why are we always arguing?" Regan asked.

"I have no idea. Why don't we count to three and we'll just kiss each other?"

She laughed softly. "All right. One—"

He didn't wait. Instead, Jamie swept her into a powerful kiss, his tongue delving deep from the moment their lips met. Regan's knees weakened, but his grip was tight around her waist as her body melted into his.

Regan had always enjoyed kissing but had never truly appreciated what a skillful kisser could make her feel. With every gentle attack and retreat, he communicated his need and escalated her own as he explored her lips, her neck, the soft skin beneath her ear.

Wild sensations raced through her body and every nerve seemed to be electrified. Regan reached for his jacket, yanking it down over his arms then tossing it aside. She fumbled with the buttons of his shirt until she was able to get it open. Smoothing her palms over his chest, she leaned into his warmth.

But a simple kiss wasn't enough anymore. As he tugged at her shirt, Regan realized that they needed each other naked.

Regan pulled him along to an old Victorian chaise along the wall, falling back onto it and dragging him down on top of her. He braced his arm beside her and unbuttoned her shirt with skilled ease. When he finally brushed aside the soft flannel, she moaned.

His fingers slipped beneath the lacy edge of her bra and Regan said a silent prayer of thanks that she'd chosen something sexy that morning. But then she remembered the plain cotton granny panties she'd been forced to choose when she couldn't find the match for her bra.

Jamie leaned forward and pressed his lips to the soft flesh he'd just exposed. Regan trembled. It had been so long since she'd been intimate with a man, she wasn't sure she could keep it together.

He ran his fingers along her collarbone, then traced a path down her body, dropping soft kisses along the way. He tugged the satin-and-lace bra back, and Regan ran her fingers through the hair at his nape and guided him to her nipple.

Jamie sucked gently and Regan lost herself in the moment, every thought focused on the spot where he lavished his attention.

Though the haze of desire, she heard the bell over the door ring, but it didn't register. A few moments later, her grandmother's voice echoed through the studio.

"Regan? Where are you?"

Jamie drew back and looked at her. He gave her a sheepish grin as he slowly crawled off her and helped her to her feet. Then, he deftly buttoned up her shirt as Regan ran her fingers through her tousled hair.

"I'll be right there, Nana," she called.

"Jamie's truck is parked out front. Is he here?"

"He is," Regan replied. "I was just giving him a tour of the studio."

"Is that what you call it?" he said softly, drawing her back into his arms. "When can I schedule another tour?"

She wriggled out of his arms. "Stop," she whispered. "Go behind that screen and button up your shirt. I'll see to my grandmother."

Regan hurried out to the gallery and found her grandmother staring at a portrait of a bride. Celia turned and smiled as Regan approached. "You do take such pretty pictures," she said.

"What are you doing here, Nana?"

"I just stopped by to let you know that I won't be home tonight. I have some business in the city and I'll be staying with your uncle David."

"What kind of business?"

"Never you mind," Ceci said. "Just a little project I've been working on."

Jamie joined the conversation. "You're not going to drive yourself." He appeared in the archway between the studio and the workroom, his clothes in perfect order. Regan's heart began to beat at a quicker tempo as she remembered what they'd shared on the chaise. Things were different now. They had a secret between the two of them.

"He's right, Nana. You shouldn't be driving that distance alone. When was the last time you drove yourself into the city?"

"Oh, I'm not driving myself. Cal Treadwell is taking me. I asked him if he would do me the favor and he said yes. He is such a lovely man. You know, he lost his wife last year."

"Before you go, I have some papers for you to sign," Jamie said. "Why don't I get them and you can sign them right here?"

Ceci waved her hand. "That will have to wait until later. Cal is waiting for me outside. Have a lovely evening."

She hurried out the front door, leaving Jamie and Regan to watch after her. "Who is Cal Treadwell?" Jamie asked.

"He's an old friend of the family. He and his wife, Millie, used to socialize with my grandparents before my grandfather died. I guess now that he's a widower, there could be something between them."

"You sound surprised."

"I am," Regan said. "When she said she wanted to start living life again, I didn't expect her to start dating!"

"I think you're missing the more important detail here."

"What's that?"

"We have the house to ourselves tonight."

"SO THIS IS what the cottage is going to look like?"

Jamie glanced across the table at Regan. He cursed beneath his breath. This was always the hardest part of the sale. Selling the look of the modules. At first blush they seem so plain, almost industrial. But once he explained how the modules functioned, people's opinions quickly changed.

"They look like shipping containers," Regan said, examining the model that he'd set in the middle of the dining table.

"Actually, you're not far off. The design is based on a shipping container. But you can put any finish on the exterior that you like. You could even make it resemble a log home."

Jamie pulled the modules apart and handed one to her. "You can arrange these any way you want. Maybe two on the bottom, one on the top, and then you can use this area as a deck."

She took the models and began to stack them in different configurations. "It's like playing with LEGO. Or Lincoln Logs. Did you have those when you were a kid?"

Jamie hadn't. There'd never been money for toys.

Occasionally, they'd find something interesting in the trash. A game of Monopoly that he'd rescued from the neighbor's garbage had been his favorite, even though it had been missing half the property cards and all the money. "Of course," he lied. "I loved Legos."

"How about this?" she asked, arranging five of the modules in a haphazard stack.

"Too high," he said. "And you have to make a spot for the stairs. They take a lot of space out of a room."

Regan arranged them again, this time in a rather artistic but abstract shape. "How about this?"

"That's actually pretty nice," he said. "You could do a nice deck here. And a walk-out to the lake on this level. We'd have to put in supports under this end, but you could use the space beneath for storage."

Regan smiled. "It really is quite easy. And you don't have to do five right away. You could do two or three and add more later."

"Of course, they'd look much nicer on Maple Point," he murmured. "It has that nice rise in the land." He paused. "You won't reconsider?"

"No. I believe I made my position clear. I'm hungry. We should think about dinner."

"Why don't you keep working on that and I'll see if I can make us something?"

"Can you cook?" Regan asked.

"I'm great at breakfast. Eggs, toast, pancakes. And I can swing pasta if you have a jar of sauce around."

"Why don't I help you?"

They chatted while they worked, mostly about Regan's childhood summers spent with her grandparents at Pickett Lake. Jamie had always known there was a better life than the one he'd lived as a child. But he'd never been able to imagine what that life might be. Regan had lived it.

"And how did you spend your summers?" Regan asked, laying plates and flatware on the table.

At first, he hadn't wanted to reveal much about his past to Regan. But suddenly he wanted her to understand where he came from. "We didn't have a lot when I was a kid."

She looked up from folding a pair of napkins. "Because of your parents' separation?"

"Because my father was killed trying to rob a gas station and because my mother was a petty criminal and a drug addict," he said.

She dropped a spoon on the table and it bounced off and clattered on the hardwood floor. Regan quickly bent and scooped it up, then slowly rose, her gaze fixed on his. "Really?"

He shrugged. "Sorry to startle you. I shouldn't have just blurted it out. I don't know why I did that." Maybe he'd hoped it would be like tearing off a bandage, easier to do in one quick rip.

"I'm glad you told me. It's sometimes best to talk about the bad things. It makes them seem less powerful."

"And what bad things do you have to tell?" Jamie asked.

"I'm not sure anything in my life would match yours. But I was left at the altar. It wasn't horrible, but it was humiliating. I walked up the aisle, dressed in my big white wedding gown. He looked at me, then he turned and ran."

Jamie groaned. "No."

She nodded. "Yes. He left me standing there, all alone, everyone staring at me, the church dead silent. Then Ceci stood up, dressed in a beautiful Chanel suit and a hat that only she could wear. She took my hand and smiled at everyone and said that though the ceremony was canceled, the reception would go on as planned—without the groom. And she sat next to me for the rest of the night and made me laugh through my tears, and convinced me that Jake's leaving me was the very best thing that could have happened."

Jamie could see it hadn't been an easy story for her to tell. Her cheeks were pink with embarrassment. "It was," he said. He brought a bowl of pasta to the table and set it in the middle. Then he moved to Regan and slipped his arms around her waist.

"How do you know?" she asked, twisting around in his arms to face him.

"Because you're here with me," Jamie said. "And you wouldn't be if you'd married…what was the idiot's name?"

"Jake," she said.

"Ah, I should have known. Guys named Jake are always idiots." He grinned. "Have you seen him since then?"

Jamie watched the play of emotion on her face as she considered her reply. It was clear that the memory of what had happened still affected her deeply. But was that because she still had feelings for this guy? He wanted to know that it was the past, that there was no love left in Regan's heart for Jake.

"His family has a big house on the other side of the lake. I've seen him from a distance a few times and we ran into each other about a year ago, around Christmas. It was—"

"Let me guess," Jamie said. "He was with his new wife. And they were shopping for the baby she's expecting."

"No!"

"His fiancée, then. And she was wearing a giant diamond ring."

Regan shook her head. "He was with his mother. And she threw her arms around me and started weeping and told me how much she missed me and how she wished I was part of their family again."

"What did you do?"

"I thanked her, then turned around and walked away. It was so awkward."

"Well, if you run into him again, give me a call. I'll take care of him."

"And what would you do?"

Jamie shrugged. "I'd make him regret what he did to you."

She pulled out a chair and sat down, tucking her leg beneath her. "No. I wouldn't want you to do that." Regan drew a deep breath. "I guess I didn't realize until now that I don't regret what he did anymore. I'm over it. It was for the best, and however painful it was at the moment, I'm over it."

He saw the tears building in her eyes and she turned

away, unwilling to let him know that the pain was still there, despite what she'd said. He wanted to drag her into his arms and kiss away the last traces of humiliation she'd felt.

"Cheese," she said, shoving away from the table. Regan hurried to the kitchen and opened the refrigerator. "We need grated cheese."

By the time she found the cheese, Jamie had already filled her plate with pasta and sauce and sat waiting for her. He poured her a glass of wine and they touched their glasses.

"To the project," she said.

"To the project," he answered.

She drew a deep breath and pasted a bright smile on her face. "How are you going to get the modules here?"

"We move the modules exactly like we move shipping containers," he began, "on trains, on ships, or in this case, on trucks. Imagine a natural disaster, where many homes are destroyed. We can load these modules onto trucks or trains, and have housing for people within a day or two."

Regan slowly nodded, riveted by the passion in his voice as he continued to talk. He really was an amazing man. But while she had the chance to enjoy a wonderful, passionate affair with him, she'd have to be very careful. It was clear his company was important to him, and once the cottage was done, he'd be on to the next thing, the next town that would help make his dream a reality.

But as long as she kept that in mind, she could stop herself from getting in too deep with him. It would all be very simple and very adult.

THEY LINGERED OVER dinner for a long time, chatting about a wide range of subjects, but keeping the conversation light and a bit silly. Jamie kept her giggling with funny stories from his boyhood.

When he finally got up to clear the table, Regan grabbed her wine and the roll of blueprints for the cottage and walked over to the stone fireplace. She spread the plans out on the floor and sat down to study them. Jamie watched her from his spot at the dining room table. They'd shared a lovely meal and it was quite pleasant to have the lodge to themselves.

She'd been tempted all night long to grab his hand and drag him into the bedroom, to continue what they'd begun earlier that afternoon in her studio. In fact, she'd barely been able to think of anything else.

Regan couldn't recall ever being this crazy about a man. She wanted to know everything about him, all the silly details…the intimate details. But that would take time, and every day that passed, the clock was ticking down.

Once he finished building the cabin, he'd go back to the city, and Regan would head south.

Jamie sat down beside her on the floor and refilled her wineglass. "What do you think?" he asked, nodding at the plans spread out in front of her.

"This is happening so fast."

He reached out and ran his fingers along her cheek. "Does that bother you?" Jamie leaned forward and brushed a kiss across her lips. "We can go slower."

"I—I was talking about the plans for the cabin. We

decided on lease terms and now we have plans. How long will it take until the project is finished?"

"Ideally only a week, depending upon the weather and how fast I work."

Regan nodded. "That's good. It will be done before I have to leave for Arizona. I've got a couple early jobs there this year. I don't want to leave Ceci with any worries while I'm gone."

"When do you usually go?"

"A few days after Christmas."

"You don't stay for New Year's Day?"

She shook her head. "I usually have a wedding on New Year's Eve. I don't this year, though. At least, not yet."

She turned her attention back to the plan and pointed to a series of circles with an X through each. "What are these?"

"Those are the trees we're going to have to remove in order to get the materials in."

"You can't cut down the trees! You didn't put that in the lease agreement. Those are my grandmother's maple trees. She loves those trees. Every spring we tap all our maples for maple syrup. It's a family tradition." Regan glanced over at him. "You're going to have to find a different way."

"I'm only clearing ten trees, and that's the bare minimum. Four of them are beneath the footprint for the cabin. I can't build on top of the trees."

Regan shook her head. "I won't change my mind."

He cursed softly. "I need a driveway and a place to park cars."

"You can put a parking lot near the road and have a path down to the cabin. It wouldn't kill people to walk."

"You want me to put in a sidewalk?"

"No," Regan said. "When we make a path in the woods we put down bark chips. It looks pretty and it's easy to walk on. You may have to build a few stairs to handle the grade down to the lake, but that shouldn't be too difficult." She held up her wineglass. "Do we have a deal?"

"I don't have any choice, do I?"

Regan smiled coyly. "You're not dealing with Nana anymore."

"I'm not finished negotiating yet," he said. Jamie took the wineglass out of her hand and set it aside. Then he grabbed her waist and dragged her down until she was stretched out beside him. He sat next to her, his hand braced along her opposite hip. "Seven maple trees. What are you willing to offer me for those trees?"

Regan giggled. "They're my trees. You're the one who needs to offer *me* something."

"Oh, right. I was confused for a second. You're such a good negotiator, you put me off my game." He drew a deep breath and let it out slowly. "For that first maple tree, I'll offer to get rid of that blouse you're wearing."

Regan pushed up on her elbows, amused at his game. "No, no. I think you ought to take off your shirt."

Without hesitation, he yanked the buttons open and tugged the shirt over his wrists, leaving him bare-chested. He handed her the shirt. "One tree, one shirt."

Regan sat up and shimmied back against the hearth, giving herself a better vantage point. If the goal was to undress him, then she'd have to work carefully. She didn't want to give up that many trees, and including his belt, he was still wearing seven items of clothing.

Regan smiled, enjoying the pleasant warmth that snaked through her body.

"What's next?" Jamie asked.

"I'm good for now. Maybe you could go get some wood for the fire? There's a stack at the end of the deck," she said. As he moved to the door, Regan watched him, her gaze taking in the details of his muscular chest and back. His abs were carved into a deep six-pack, and deep groves marked the muscles over his hips.

Her cheeks felt hot and she moved away from the fire and waited for Jamie to return. Was she prepared to seduce him? She reminded herself that she'd had a few casual relationships, and this would be no different. She wanted no-strings, no-regrets sex. And when she left for Arizona, she'd kiss him goodbye and be perfectly happy with her choice.

That sounded like a good plan. But could she really keep her feelings in check? It was already hard enough to kiss Jamie without going all gooey inside. If she couldn't be sure she wouldn't get hurt, then she shouldn't take things any further with him.

He struggled with the door, then stepped back inside, his arms piled with wood. His biceps flexed and a shiver skittered down her spine as she thought about how those arms would feel wrapped around her body.

Regan closed her eyes and drew a deep breath. Self-control.

After feeding the fire, Jamie grabbed pillows from

the sofa and scattered them around. He followed the pillows with a pair of quilts that were usually thrown over the back of the wing chairs.

"There," he said. "How's that?"

Regan smiled. "Perfect."

"Should we get back to our game?"

She frowned. "Game?"

"Yes. Your attempt to separate me from my clothing by way of your maple trees."

"Oh, right. What would I get for just one more tree?"

"My shoes and socks," he said. He quickly took them off and tossed them aside. Jamie leaned forward and kissed her. "Now what?"

Suddenly, she wasn't sure of herself. He seemed to be waiting for her to make all the moves and Regan didn't know what came next. Her hand trembled as she reached for her wine, and the glass tipped over and splattered onto her shirt.

"Oh, no," she murmured.

"Take it off," he said. "I'll rinse it in cold water." Jamie reached for the buttons, but Regan drew back. The impulse made her doubts clear. She wasn't ready to do this. She wasn't ready to shed her clothes and surrender to his touch. She wasn't sure how she felt about him or whether she could keep herself from falling in love.

"It's late," she murmured, getting to her feet. "I'm tired and I should get to bed. I have a busy day tomorrow."

Jamie stared at her for a long moment, his gaze scanning her features for a clue to her sudden change of heart. "Sure," he finally said. "Go ahead. I'll put out the fire and finish cleaning up." He drew a deep breath. "Sleep tight."

"You, too." Regan hurried out of the great room and up the stairs to her bedroom. Her heart pounded in her chest and she paused to catch her breath. When she heard him moving downstairs, she continued on to her bedroom, closing the door behind her.

She'd let a wolf inside the house, and now he was on the verge of consuming her. She'd kept her grandmother safe, but what about her? Was it too late?

She threw herself on the bed and pulled the covers over her head. Tomorrow morning she'd know what to do. She'd get a good night's sleep and everything would be much clearer in the morning.

5

JAMIE RAKED HIS hands through his damp hair as he jogged down the stairs to the kitchen. The sun had been up for nearly an hour, but he'd lingered in bed, putting together a mental list of the tasks that had to be completed that day. He also spent a fair amount of time wondering what was going to happen next with Regan.

After last night, he wasn't quite sure where they were headed. Their silly little game had seemed like a good warm-up to seduction. But then something had happened and Regan had called an end to it. One moment she'd seemed ready to throw herself into a passionate affair, and the next moment, the doubts had crept in.

In truth, Jamie was having doubts of his own. His sex life consisted of a series of one-night, sometimes two-night, stands. But he always chose women who didn't appeal to him intellectually. For Jamie, smart women were dangerous. They provided a challenge that he couldn't resist. And the harder he tried, the harder he fell.

It had happened only a few times in his life—once in college, and again about three years ago. On both occasions, he'd found himself blindsided by his romantic feelings. And he'd been the one to get hurt.

Was it any wonder that the thought of love frightened him? He had no reference point, no way to judge the truth of his feelings. He could offer Regan passion and physical release, but he didn't know how to offer her his heart. She'd said she didn't want his heart, but her reaction last night seemed to show that she had as many doubts about them being able to pull off a strictly physical affair as he did.

When he got to the kitchen, a pot of coffee was already brewing. He grabbed a mug and poured himself a cup, then walked over to the fireplace and scooped up the plans that Regan had left there the night before. Celia still hadn't signed the lease offer, but he decided to push ahead with the plans rather than wait. Regan had agreed to the terms, so he didn't expect any more problems. Celia was due back the next day. The signatures could wait until then.

Jamie set the plans on the end of the counter and then poured another cup of coffee, adding a measure of sugar to it, as he'd seen Regan do for herself. He knew how she took her coffee and how she liked her eggs, that she preferred red wine over white, and real butter over margarine. It was more than he'd ever discovered about most of the women he'd slept with—and he hadn't slept with Regan yet.

He slowly walked up the stairs, a cup of coffee in each hand. When he reached Regan's bedroom door, he found it slightly ajar. Pushing the door open with his foot, he peeked inside, expecting to find her curled up in bed. Instead, he found it empty, as was the adjoining bathroom.

Jamie walked over to her bed and set the hot coffee down on the nightstand. He reached out to straighten the pillow, then picked it up and pressed it to his face, inhaling deeply. The scent of her hair filled his head and he smiled. He couldn't identify the exact smell, only that it was something floral.

Setting his coffee down next to hers, he walked into the bathroom in search of her shampoo. He found the bottle in the shower and grabbed it, holding it to his nose. "That's it," he murmured to himself.

As he walked out of the bathroom with the bottle, Jamie read the label. "Lavender," he said, sniffing again.

"What are you doing?"

Regan came out of the closet dressed in jeans and a canvas jacket. Rubber boots covered her feet and calves and her hair was hidden beneath a knit cap. She looked beautiful. Jamie scrambled for an explanation for why he held the bottle. "I—I brought you coffee. And when you weren't here, I remembered that I needed shampoo. I wanted to see if you had any."

"You're stealing my shampoo?" she asked.

"I was going to borrow it. But it smells a little girlie." He held it out to her. Regan stepped forward and took it from his hand, regarding him suspiciously. "Is there anything else you need?"

"Not that I can think of," Jamie said. "Maybe a little breakfast?"

"Get your jacket. You'll want gloves and a hat, too. It's really chilly this morning. We'll grab something to eat on the way out."

"Where are we going?"

She smiled, tossing the shampoo on the bed and grabbing her coffee. "You'll see." She walked to the door, then turned around. "Can you swim?"

"Yeah, I can swim."

"Okay, then, let's go."

Jamie followed Regan downstairs. She made him a couple toaster waffles, then wrapped them up in foil. Next, she transferred their coffee into travel mugs and handed him his.

When they got outside, the air was still and a faint mist hung over the lake. They walked down to the shore and Jamie noticed a canoe pulled up on the narrow sand beach. He watched as Regan stowed her coffee, then shoved the canoe into the shallow water. "Get in," she said. "You can take the seat up front. Be careful. It will be wobbly."

Jamie glanced back at her. "Wobbly?"

"Have you ever been in a canoe?"

"I've been in a kayak," he said. "Does that count?"

"Not really. Just be careful not to move too much. And once you're sitting, stay sitting."

Jamie stepped inside, then slowly made his way forward. Regan was right. Every shift of his weight made the canoe rock wildly. And they were in only a few feet of water. He wedged his coffee mug into a spot between the seat and the hull and then sat down.

"Put that life jacket on," she said.

"I can swim," he said. Jamie turned to see that Regan had already donned a life jacket herself.

"The water is too cold. If we swamp the canoe, we won't be able to get back inside. We'll have to swim to shore, and without a jacket, you won't make it."

Jamie snatched up the life vest and slipped his arms into it, then snapped the front buckles. "All right, Captain, tell me what to do."

Regan pushed the canoe out into deeper water, then gracefully hopped inside, settling herself in the rear seat. She grabbed a paddle from the floor of the canoe and began to stroke in a slow rhythm, shifting sides after two deep pulls in the dark water.

He stared out at the lake, taking in the eerie sight of the mist rising up from the cold water. "Where are we going?" he asked over his shoulder.

"I thought it would be nice for you to get a look at your property from this view. You'll want the cottage to look good from here, since this is the side people will see from their boats."

She paddled north along the shore and then farther out into the lake. "This space is a little more open," she said. "Not as heavily wooded."

"Were the trees cut?"

"Probably. Long ago. But it has a nice little beach. And that rock outcropping is pretty."

"I guess it will work. It's not as pretty as Maple Point. Let's paddle over there."

She turned the canoe around and headed south along the shore, the paddle dipping smoothly into the water.

They glided past the lodge and then along the heavily wooded shore of Maple Point.

She let the canoe drift as she caught movement in the trees. "Look," she said.

Jamie swung his legs over the seat, attempting to face her, but the canoe rocked wildly. He grabbed the edge and leaned forward in an attempt to balance them, but it only made things worse.

"Stop," she said, holding out her hand. "Move slowly. Balance yourself as you go along."

He nodded and slowly pulled his other leg over the seat. "What are we looking at?"

"There." A doe and her fawn cautiously emerged from the trees. They walked to the water's edge, then dipped their noses into the water and drank. Regan held her breath, automatically reaching for her camera. But she hadn't brought it along. She pulled out her phone and quietly snapped a few shots.

"Now that was pretty cool," he said.

"Almost as cool as those foxes you scared away," she teased.

Jamie reached inside his jacket and pulled out the waffles she'd made. He took one from the foil, then tossed the second one toward her. Unfortunately, his aim was off and the waffle plopped into the water. A few seconds later, a family of ducks paddled out from the shore and enjoyed the breakfast he'd provided.

"Sorry," he said. "You can have this one."

Regan shook her head. "I had breakfast earlier. You eat it."

They drifted around the end of the point and into a

small bay. Regan had to admit Maple Point was a much prettier spot than the land he'd agreed to take. But his cabin was just a model. No one would live there, so what did the view matter?

Maybe she ought to change her mind. After all, if she liked the home he built, then she wouldn't have to worry about building a place of her own. And if it wasn't what she wanted, at the end of the lease he was required to demolish it. Five years wasn't that long.

"It is a beautiful piece of property," Jamie said. "I don't blame you for turning me down."

"You don't?"

He shook his head. "No. It's your land. Your decision."

"But now that I see it, I was thinking that your cottage would look the best if it were set into that rise. You could clear the brush from the water to the cottage and that would improve the view. You'd want to keep the privacy of the trees, but you'd have a view of the water."

He nodded. "But that's not on the table. Can we paddle back to the other spot?"

"There's a paddle under your feet. Why don't you grab it and we'll get there faster."

He reached for it, but the canoe rocked precariously. Holding out his arms, Jamie stopped. "This is like a metaphor for our relationship," he muttered.

"What?"

"Nothing," Jamie said.

"I heard what you said. Why is this canoe a metaphor for us?"

"Because it is constantly off balance," Jamie said.

"Always in danger of capsizing. And I never seem to get to paddle."

She gasped. "That's not true."

"Oh, yes, it is. You have been in the driver's seat from the very start. And I've been all right with that. But a man can only take so much. There are moments when I feel like tipping the damn canoe over and walking away."

"Swimming away," she corrected.

"Whatever." He took a bite of the waffle. "So, are we going to talk about what happened last night?"

"For a guy, you sure do like to talk about things. Isn't that supposed to be a girl thing?"

"You're avoiding the issue. Do you want to explain what scared you last night?"

Regan shrugged. "We haven't known each other that long. And I prefer to be careful about matters of the heart."

"This is most definitely a matter of the body," he said. "Remember, as you made clear, we're not letting our hearts get involved."

"You know what I mean."

"Maybe I should move into the guest cottage," Jamie said. "It would probably make things easier if we weren't living under the same roof."

"Ceci will be back tomorrow," Regan said. "She'll serve as a chaperone."

"If that's the way you want it, I promise to keep my hands to myself until then," Jamie said. "And my lips. They sometimes get me into trouble."

Regan laughed. "I can see why," she said. "Maybe

you should just keep your hand over your mouth when you're around me and I won't be tempted, either."

"But I want to tempt you," Jamie said. He braced his hands on the edges of the canoe and leaned forward. "I can tell you want to kiss me right now. Either that, or you want my waffle."

"The waffle," Regan said. She raised the paddle from the water and held it out in front of her. "If you move, you'll dump us both in the water."

"I've got it now," Jamie said, leaning forward to drop the half-eaten waffle on the blade of her paddle. But at the last moment, the shift of his weight rocked the canoe. Regan moved her paddle back to the water, slapping the waffle overboard.

Jamie's instinctually tried to save her breakfast, but the sudden movement was more than the canoe could take. He fell against the edge and Regan screamed. A moment later, the canoe was upside down and they were both in the water.

THE SHOCK FROM the cold water took Regan's breath away. The life jacket kept her afloat, and luckily, they were only twenty yards from shore. "Jamie!"

He didn't answer at first but she could hear him splashing on the other side of the canoe. Regan swam around the bow and found him treading water, a soggy waffle in his left hand.

"Throw that away," she cried.

He pitched it behind him and then swam over to her. "Sorry. My bad."

Regan shook her head. "You're damn right it's your bad. Come on, we need to get out of this water."

"I think I can get the canoe upright," Jamie said.

"Don't bother. It's not worth the waste of energy. We'll just pull it to shore and leave it there. The faster we get home, the better off we'll be."

Regan swam to the bow again and found the rope that she usually used to tie the canoe up. Her clothes were heavy with water, but thanks to the life jacket she managed to make quick progress toward shore, the line cast over her shoulder. Within a minute her feet were on solid ground and two minutes later she was struggling to drag the canoe onto the rocky point. Jamie joined her, lifting the end up and pulling the craft ashore. Obviously exhausted, he sat down in the brush, gasping for breath.

Regan held out her hand and when he took it she pulled him to his feet. "Come on. We have to keep moving or hypothermia will set it."

"I'm all right," he said. "It's not too bad."

"The air temperature is close to freezing and your clothes are sucking the heat out of your body faster than you can generate it. We've got about fifteen minutes before the shivering starts, and it's about a ten minute walk to the lodge. Let's go."

Regan had two options. They could walk along the water's edge, where the footing was easier but the trip was longer. Or they could cut across the point, crawling through the dense underbrush until they found a path. Her teeth were already chattering and she was afraid the last of her energy would be drained out of her if they had to work too hard to get through the brush.

"We'll follow the shore," she ordered.

"Wouldn't it be faster to cut through the woods?" he asked.

Regan drew a shaky breath, then shook her head. "No. I—I mean, yes. We'll go through the woods." She looked along the shoreline, searching for someplace familiar. Along this stretch there should be a narrow footpath, but she didn't have time to find it.

Before she could say anything else, Jamie grabbed her and wrapped her in his arms. He ran his hands over her back, rubbing and patting, as if that would warm her, then bent over to gaze into her eyes. "Are you all right?"

"Fine. I just want to get back to the lodge and get out of these wet clothes." Regan started into the woods, pushing aside the brush as she searched for decent footing across the rough terrain. Between the rocks and her frozen limbs, it was almost impossible to stay upright.

The search for the trail was growing more exhausting by the minute. By now, Regan couldn't feel her fingers or her toes, and she was starting to lose the ability to think rationally. She wanted to sit down and rest, but she knew it would be impossible to get up again. She looked back at Jamie, who seemed to be coping with the cold much better than her. When he saw her face, a worried expression across his handsome features.

Jamie reached out and grabbed her arm, pulling her to a stop. He uttered a vivid curse and cupped her face in his hands. "Your lips are blue!"

"I'm cold," Regan said. A shudder racked her body and her teeth chattered. Regan took a step forward, pulling herself from his grasp. But Jamie wouldn't have it. He stepped in front of her and began to make a trail, pushing aside the brush so she could pass. They walked another ten yards and the path appeared before them. Regan sighed with relief. Walking would be so much easier now. She rubbed her fingers together to restore circulation, but they were painfully stiff. She pulled off the sodden gloves and shoved them in her pockets.

Jamie stopped, then patted his back. "Hop on," he said. "We can move much faster if I carry you."

"Don't be ridiculous," she said. "I can make it on my own."

They continued through the woods, Regan's legs numb inside the half-frozen jeans she wore. When they finally reached the manicured lawn of the lodge, Regan sat down on the ground and yanked off her boots and socks. Without them, her toes felt instantly warmer. She increased her tempo, striding through the grass, the damp strands soft beneath her feet.

When they finally reached the lodge, Jamie jogged ahead of her and pulled the door open. Regan hurried inside. The moment she entered the warmth of the house, she began to strip off her clothes, tossing each item aside. As she climbed the stairs to the second floor, she tugged off her T-shirt, leaving herself in just her bra and panties.

She turned around and found him standing at the base of the stairs, watching her with a bemused expression. "Well? Get your clothes off. You're never going to get warm that way."

"Where are you going?" Jamie asked.

"The steam shower in your bedroom," she said.

He followed her up the stairs. "I don't think that's a good idea," he said. "You're not supposed to take a shower if there's a possibility you might be hypothermic."

She stood in the middle of the bedroom, shivering. "What am I supposed to do then?"

Jamie walked to the closet, pulled out a down blanket and wrapped it around her shoulders. "Take off your wet underwear."

Regan did as she was told. Then, without warning, he stripped out of his boxers and pulled the comforter around his body, as well. He hugged her close, rubbing her back and arms. "See, we use our body heat to warm each other up."

"I'm not that cold anymore," she said.

"Neither am I. But this is kind of nice, don't you think?"

"I think you're making this up," she said.

Jamie pulled her along to the bed and they tumbled down onto the mattress together, still wrapped in the comforter. He reached out and snatched his phone from the bedside table. "I'm not, and I'll prove it to you." When he found a website saying what to do if you have hypothermia, he handed her the phone. "We need to snuggle underneath this blanket until our core temperature returns to normal."

Regan wasn't sure how long they spent wrapped in

the comforter. But gradually, her body warmed against his, from the tips of her fingers to the tips of her toes. She pressed her face into his chest. "I think we're safe from hypothermia now," she murmured. "I'm going to take a shower. My hair smells like the lake."

When she reached his bathroom, she switched on the control panel and set the timer for steam. Then she stepped inside and turned on the full complement of jets and showerheads, adjusting the water temperature until it was comfortable.

She stepped inside, pulling the door shut behind her. The warm water poured over her body and she groaned as it chased away the last of the cold. Regan heard the door open behind her and she glanced over her shoulder and smiled at Jamie.

He slipped his arms around her waist and pulled her body against his. Regan closed her eyes, her heart skipping a beat as he pressed his lips to her shoulder. When they'd been wrapped in the blanket, he'd been strictly focused on getting her warm again. But now, his intentions had clearly changed.

"I'm sorry for tipping the canoe," he said. "But I'm not sorry we get to warm up like this."

Regan turned to face him then sat on the teak bench. Steam slowly filled the shower and she watched him though a haze. She slid to the end of the bench, silently offering him a place to sit. "I was cold to the bone. I don't think I've been that cold since I was a kid."

"Did you fall in the water?"

"No. My grandfather used to clear a patch of ice for us on the lake. Then he'd plow a long, winding path all the way out to the point and back. We used to skate for hours. We'd come in and put on our flannel pajamas and sit in front of the fire all wrapped up in blankets. My grandmother would give us hot cocoa to warm us up. I like this method much better."

"We'll have to go skating this winter."

"You skate?"

"Yeah, I played a little hockey with my brothers. I was a decent skater, but couldn't handle the puck very well. They always put me in goal and I'd just take pucks to the helmet for two or three hours. It was never much fun."

"I promise I won't do that."

"How do your toes feel?" Jamie picked up her foot. He bent close and took her toes into his warm mouth.

Regan gasped at the wave of sensation that washed over her. She'd never considered her feet an erogenous zone, but his tongue was proving her wrong. "What are you doing?"

"Warming you up," he said.

A shiver skittered through her body, but it wasn't from the cold. The mood had shifted and she suddenly felt vulnerable, yet filled with anticipation.

Jamie had said that he was growing tired of the instability in their relationship, and Regan was, too. She wanted this. She wanted him.

She'd changed from the naive young woman who'd been jilted at the altar. She was stronger, wiser. And she'd proved that she could have a no-strings relationship without involving her heart. Jamie would be no different.

She drew a deep breath, then swung her legs off his lap and stood up. Her hands trembled and she stepped beneath the hot water again, letting it rush over her face and body.

Her heart slammed in her chest and she silently counted the beats, waiting for him to make the next move. What if he didn't? What if he just stepped out of the shower and walked away? Jilted at the altar was one thing, but jilted while stark naked in a shower could be even worse.

She jumped when his fingers came to rest on her shoulder. His hand trailed down her arm to her hip, and she let go of a tightly held breath. His touch seemed amplified by the water, as if every nerve were alive and waiting to react.

Jamie gently turned her around to face him. She looked up, fascinated by the droplets that clung to his long, dark lashes. With a soft moan, she wrapped her arms around his neck and kissed him, pushing up on her toes until their lips fit perfectly together.

His hands skimmed over her face as his tongue invaded her mouth. He seemed desperate to taste her, and Regan hoped that was the way he'd take her body. She drew a ragged breath as his lips moved down to her shoulder, her breast, and finally, to her nipple.

He grabbed her hands and held them above her head as he pressed her back against the wall of the shower, his hips against hers. His shaft was hard and hot against her belly.

Her doubts were gone, replaced by a deep instinct

that drove her toward pleasure. As he nuzzled her breast, Regan dragged his hand down between her legs.

"Yes," he said, his voice barely audible above the falling water. "That's what you want."

His fingers seduced her—determined and desperate to please. He spread her legs and slipped a finger between the soft folds of flesh, gently probing until he found the right spot.

Regan's knees went weak and she clutched his shoulders in an attempt to remain upright. His free arm slipped around her waist as he continued to caress her. Regan allowed herself to surrender to the waves of pleasure that coursed through her body.

He knew exactly what he was doing, drawing her close to the edge, then pulling her back. Each time, the sensations grew more and more intense and the anticipation more difficult to deny.

Suddenly, out of nowhere, the first spasm hit. She tried to control the free fall, but her body betrayed her and she dissolved in deep, uncontrollable shudders. Regan cried out, her fingertips digging into his shoulders.

It took a long time for the effects of her orgasm to subside. He kissed her softly, whispering soothing words against her damp lips. "Nice shower."

"Next time I'll have to show you how to use all the features," she said.

"There was only one feature I was really interested in," Jamie said. "You."

Regan shut off the water, and when she opened the glass door, the steam billowed into the bathroom, creating another thick haze. She grabbed a towel from the cabinet beside the sink and handed it to him, but he reached out and wrapped it around her body, pulling her close.

"Are you warm now?" he murmured.

She nodded. "To the bone." She reached down and gently wrapped her fingers around his erection, still slick from the shower. "What about you?"

"I'm getting there," he whispered.

REGAN PULLED HIM along behind her to the bed and they fell down onto the comforter, their damp bodies still slick against each other, their mouths melding. It was clear to them both that they'd waited long enough. She straddled his hips and moved back and forth along the length of his shaft, teasing him with the damp warmth between her legs.

Jamie grabbed the box of condoms from the bedside table and handed them to her. She gave him a smug smile. "When did you buy these?"

"The day after I met you," he said.

"You knew we'd end up here?"

He nodded. "Yeah. I did."

She laughed as she tore open the package and smoothed the latex over his shaft. Then he pulled her beneath him and in one smooth motion, slipped inside her.

Just the feel of her warmth surrounding him was enough to put him on the edge of release. He drew a deep breath and tried to regain control. He braced his hands on either side of her shoulders, staring down into her flushed face.

"Move," she whispered.

He smiled and shook his head. "Not yet."

She moaned softly, arching her hips to meet his. The movement brought him closer to the edge of his self-control, but he managed to keep it in check. He'd waited for this moment since he'd met her, and now that it had come, he didn't want it to end.

He reached down and pulled her thigh up along his hip, still buried deep inside her. Leaning closer, he brushed his lips across hers, the tip of his tongue following the crease.

"Why do you torture me?" she asked. Regan reached up and wrapped her hand around his nape, then yanked him into a deep and desperate kiss.

His body reacted instinctively and he plunged deeper within her, then slowly withdrew. He couldn't help himself. The need to feel her surrender was all he wanted. He'd brought her close, but was she ready to step off the edge?

He pressed deep again, stretching his body out above hers. And then, grabbing her waist, Jamie rolled over, settling her on top of him, her legs straddling his waist.

"Move," he said.

A satisfied smile curled the corners of her mouth and she did. Rocking above him, Regan's body was open to his gaze and to his touch. He reached out and cupped her breast, smoothing his thumb over the taut nipple.

Every inch of her fascinated him. He could spend a lifetime exploring the intricacies of her body. Jamie drew her breast into his mouth, his tongue teasing her nipple. He heard her breath catch in her throat and he knew she was close. He fixed his gaze on her face, then reached between them and touched the damp folds between her legs.

Regan cried out as he found the spot, then suddenly stopped moving. They both stayed frozen for a long moment. He grabbed her hip, giving one last thrust. And in a heartbeat, they both tumbled off the edge, reality blurring into a rush of sensation and pure pleasure. Regan collapsed on his chest, gasping for breath, and he waited for his own sweet agony to subside.

Jamie kissed the top of her head and closed his eyes, his body completely spent. "If we keep this up, I'll never get around to building that cottage," he joked.

She pushed off his chest and met his gaze, a frown creasing her brow. "That'll go over big with your business partners."

"I'm not worried yet. Materials should arrive tomorrow or the next day. Once I get everything sorted out, I can get started." His stomach growled and he smiled at her. "What time is it? How long until Ceci gets back?"

Regan rolled over and grabbed his phone from the bedside table, then rested her chin on his chest as she dialed.

"What are you doing?"

"Calling to get my messages."

"Where is your phone?"

"It was in my jacket pocket when I went in the lake." She paused. "There's a message from Nana. She's going to stay another night. So we have the house to ourselves again."

"Well, we know what we're not going to do," Jamie said. "No more canoeing."

"I'm a very good canoeist. You're just a horrible passenger."

"Personally, I think you planned the whole thing. Just to get me naked and into bed," Jamie said, ruffling her hair with his hand.

She pressed her palms against his chest, putting him at arm's length. "Do you really believe I'd do something like that?"

Jamie slowly shook his head. He didn't know much about Regan, but he was sure she wasn't the type to manipulate a man to get what she wanted. He liked that about her. She didn't play games. She said exactly what she meant and wasn't afraid to disagree with him. In truth, he'd never met a woman quite as sure of what she wanted as Regan.

"No, you'd never do that," he said with a sleepy smile. Jamie stretched his arms over his head. "Aren't you hungry?"

Regan held up his phone and snapped a photo of him. "I could eat." She showed him the screen. "That was a good one. That's definitely bed head there. Post-coital hair."

He grabbed the camera and took a photo of her, then showed it to her. Regan screamed. "I look like a witch."

Jamie shook his head. "You look beautiful."

She took the phone back and tapped the phone again. Regan admired the picture she'd taken and sighed. "You have a face that's made for photographs," she said. "Symmetry. Almost a perfect balance to your features."

Regan held out the camera for him to see the photo and Jamie shrugged.

She pushed a few more buttons and then showed him the picture again. "See? I split the photo in half and put a mirror image of one half against itself. It's the same as the original. That's why so many women find you attractive."

"What women find me attractive?" Jamie asked. Laughing, he grabbed the phone. "Do you find me attractive?"

"Of course I do. You're very handsome."

Regan glanced over at him and smiled. "Look at you. You're blushing. I need to get a shot of this."

"How long have you been taking photos?"

"As long as I can remember. I got a digital camera for Christmas when I was about five or six years old. I still have that camera." She pulled her knees up under her chin and wrapped her arms around her legs, her gaze still fixed on his picture. "But I didn't always take pictures of logical subjects. I remember once when my mother asked me to take a photo of our house. I came back with an image of the front doorknob."

"Just the doorknob?"

Regan nodded. "It seemed to say home to me. It's the first thing you touch when you arrive. Everyone touches it. If you take a photo of the entire house, you miss the emotional power of what the pieces say."

"That makes sense," he said.

"My grandmother says I prefer to watch the world through my camera because that's the only way I can control the world. I choose when to snap the shutter, how long to wait for the light, what angle to choose."

"Is it true?"

She shrugged. "My grandmother knows me better than anyone, so maybe it is." Regan scrambled back on the bed, then motioned to him. "Lie down on your stomach."

He groaned. "No more photos.

"I want to show you something," Regan said softly.

He waited as she took three more photos. "Done?"

She nodded. "A lot of photographers feel that digital photography has ruined the art. That fine art photography should be about the purity of the image. You know, kind of like the battle between CDs and vinyl. Old school versus new technology."

Jamie rolled onto his side, bracing his arm beneath his head. "And what do you think?"

"I like the freedom of digital photography. It allows me to create layers of art, finding a way to make an image even more interesting. My big break came when I photographed my cousin's wedding and her photos appeared in a local bridal magazine. From that moment on, I was a professional photographer."

He watched her as she stared at his phone, wondering what she saw in the photo she'd just taken. "What are you doing?"

"Just messing with it. Hold on. Be patient."

Finally, she handed him the phone. She'd taken a photo of his arm, twisted in the sheet of the bed. At first, he wasn't sure what she'd intended to convey. But then he saw the tension in his arm, the way his hand gripped the sheet. Pleasure. That moment when everything came together.

"I understand," he whispered.

It wasn't just sex they'd shared. And it wasn't all about physical release. She'd caught an emotion with her camera, an emotion that he was just beginning to recognize.

6

REGAN BURROWED INTO the covers of Jamie's bed, nuzzling her face into his shoulder. She was perfectly comfortable, her naked limbs warm beneath the thick duvet. They'd spent an entire day together, moving between the bed and the kitchen and a roaring fire in the hearth. She smiled to herself. It had been the perfect way to spend a cold and rainy day.

She opened her eyes and peered out from beneath the bed linens. The weather had improved and today the sun shone through the windows. Regan sat up and rubbed the sleep from her eyes, then glanced over at Jamie.

He slept on his stomach, his face buried in the pillow and his arms thrown out across the width of the bed. She studied him closely, wondering at the pure intimacy of the moment. A week ago they'd been strangers, and now they were lovers, sharing a bed as if it were the most natural thing in the world.

She pressed her lips to his shoulder, drawing a deep breath. Regan couldn't help but wonder if they'd share a bed tonight or the next night. They didn't have much time before they had to go their separate ways.

Her stomach growled and she glanced over at the clock. It was already half past eight. Careful not to disturb Jamie, Regan crawled out of bed and grabbed the quilt, then wrapped it around her body.

Her grandmother was due back later that afternoon. Once she was home, she'd expect proper behavior from her granddaughter and her houseguest. But then, maybe she'd left them alone together on purpose.

Regan raked her fingers through her tangled hair as she walked to the bedroom door. She glanced over her shoulder once more, taking in the sight of Jamie warm and naked—and for the moment, all hers.

As she walked downstairs, her mind rewound the events from the previous forty-eight hours. She'd been so worried about taking the next step with him. He'd been sweet and passionate and eager to please her. And though she'd had her share of sexual experiences with men, it was clear that he'd actually learned a few very important things that her previous lovers had never bothered to figure out.

When she reached the bottom of the stairs, the scent of coffee touched her nose. Regan frowned, wondering how Jamie had managed to rise without waking her. But to her surprise, she found her grandmother in the kitchen with a handsome, elderly gentleman.

"Hello, darling. You've slept late. Can I get you a cup of coffee? You remember Cal Treadwell, don't you?"

Regan scrambled to put together answers. "Nana! What are you doing here?"

"I live here," she said, a twinkle in her eye. "I should ask what you're doing here…dressed in nothing but one of my antique quilts." She winked at Cal.

"I should get a move on," Cal said.

Regan watched as he stood and crossed to Ceci, then planted a kiss on her cheek. She whispered something in his ear and he smiled. "I'll call you," he murmured.

"I'll be waiting," Ceci said, giving him a coy wave.

Regan stared at her grandmother, waiting for the front door to swing shut. As soon as it did, she leaned forward, her elbows on the granite countertop. "What is going on here?"

"What do you mean?" Ceci asked.

"Let's start with your hair. We just had it done a few days ago and now it's completely different."

"I know. I saw a photo in a magazine and wanted to try it. It's very Helen Mirren."

In truth, the hairstyle was…sexy, a tumble of platinum waves that fell around Ceci's face and made her look at least twenty years younger. And her nail polish was no longer the frosted pink that Regan had chosen a few days ago, but a flaming red.

"And you and Cal are…?"

Ceci's pale cheeks flushed a pretty pink. "I'm not sure. I suppose we're—" she thought about her answer for a moment "—exploring our options."

"Nana! Are you sleeping with him?"

Her eyebrows shot up and she shook her head. "No. Of course not. Not…yet." Suddenly, her eyes filled with tears. "But I'm not going to let anyone stop me from seeing him. And I don't want you to think that I'm being disloyal to your grandfather. I still love him with all my heart, but before he died, he made me promise that I wouldn't spend the rest of my days all alone." She brushed away a tear. "I suppose I have Jamie to thank for all of this."

"Jamie?"

Ceci nodded. "I'll admit that I noticed he was a handsome man. And I imagined what it might be like to have a handsome man in my life again. Of course, Jamie is far too young for me, but I stumbled across Cal on Facebook and remembered how much fun he was. I sent him a note and here we are."

Regan reached out and covered her grandmother's hand. "Everyone wants you to be happy, Ceci."

"No, they don't. You'll see. The family would prefer I stayed home and didn't cause them any worry. But I've decided that if I have any years left, I'm going to live my life exactly the way I want to."

"Good for you!"

"Hey, Regan?"

The sound of Jamie's voice echoed through the lodge.

"In here," she called, then said a silent prayer that he'd walk in fully dressed. When he appeared wearing just his boxers, she groaned inwardly. If it wasn't obvious what was going on between them now, then Ceci was just oblivious.

Jamie stopped short when he saw her grandmother. He glanced over at Regan and forced a smile. "Excuse me. I'm just going to—"

"Oh, sit down," Ceci said, waving at the stool next to her.

Regan hurried over to one of the wing chairs in the great room and retrieved a small throw, dropping it in his lap as she returned to the kitchen.

He handed her the replacement phone she'd picked up in town yesterday. "Something must be going on with your family," he said. "Your phone started ringing about ten minutes ago and it hasn't stopped since."

She grabbed her phone and scanned the screen. Six calls from various members of her family—her father, her two sisters, her uncle and a cousin.

"Ignore them for now. I'm glad you're both here," Ceci said. "I need to talk to you about our agreement. I'd like to make some changes."

Regan looked at Jamie and saw the concern in his eyes. "Nana, we already agreed on leasing the land north of the lodge. We can't go back on that now."

"I don't intend to. I spent yesterday with my financial advisor and I'm ready to invest in Habikit. Which means I won't require you to pay a leasing fee. That will be part of my investment. Along with another quarter million." She withdrew a check from the folder and held it out to Jamie. "I've had an offer drawn up for you to discuss with your partners."

Regan took the check from her grandmother. "Nana, maybe you need time to think about this."

"I have thought about it. I'm determined to start living life again. I want to get involved in the world. And now Jamie can use the money to make sure his company is on solid ground to be able to do more good."

"But investing in Habikit is a risk," Jamie said. "I can afford to take that risk. I'm not sure you can."

"Well, my financial advisor disagrees. As soon as you accept my offer, then you can get started."

"I need to make a few calls," Jamie said. "Maybe you and Regan can discuss this in greater detail." He sent Regan a hesitant smile, but she wasn't sure how to respond. Leasing the land was one thing. But investing good money in a risky venture was another.

She waited for Jamie to leave the room, then focused on her grandmother. "I don't think this is a good idea. Leasing the land to him is enough involvement for you. Wait and see how things go before you take another step."

Ceci shook her head. "I'm decided."

"But why?" Regan stared at her for a long moment. Was this some sort of gesture of gratitude for getting Ceci back out into the world? What other reason could she—

The realization hit Regan like a slap to the face. "No," she murmured. "Are you doing this for me?"

"For you?"

"Are you buying me a boyfriend? Oh, Nana, don't even think of that."

"I hadn't," Ceci said. "But I suppose that might be an unintended benefit of my investment. Particularly since I had planned to turn this all over to you to supervise, so that would—"

"No! Don't you dare try to play matchmaker. I will never forgive you."

Ceci smiled. "So you really care about this man."

"No. We're just…oh, I don't know. And it doesn't make any difference. I'm leaving town in a month and he'll go back to his life and we'll never see each other again."

"It's me you're talking to, darling. I know you better than you know yourself."

Tears pressed at the corners of Regan's eyes as frustration built within her. But she wouldn't allow herself to cry. "Don't do this. It's…it's humiliating."

Ceci smiled. "Darling, don't overthink this. Just follow your heart and everything will be fine."

"I'm not going to marry him, Nana. It doesn't matter how financially secure he is. We're not going to have a future together. We've both agreed on this. It's not just me."

Her grandmother gave her an odd look. "Why would you agree to something like that?"

"Because not everyone is supposed to have a happily ever after," she said. "For us, it's just happily until it's over."

"You could always change your mind." She circled the island and pressed a kiss to Regan's cheek. "He seems like a wonderful man. Give him a chance."

Regan watched her grandmother walk out of the room. Ceci seemed so happy, so full of energy and optimism. But there was no way Regan was changing her mind.

She didn't want any tearstained, desperately messy endings with him. When it was over, they'd go their separate ways and be happy about it.

She ripped the check into tiny pieces and then threw it in the garbage bin. Jamie would have to do without.

JAMIE PULLED HIS truck to a stop at the curb and put it into Park. He'd finished up his business in the city and was supposed to meet his brother, Tristan, for a drink in an hour. He'd thought about grabbing some dinner, but didn't relish the prospect of eating alone. So he had some time to kill.

His brothers' favorite watering hole was not far from their old neighborhood. For some reason, he was drawn there, curious about the old house that they'd lived in for two or three years.

The neighborhood had gentrified over the past twenty years, and houses that had once been run-down were now nicely painted. A light behind the window of his old first-floor bedroom allowed him to see the room's brightly painted walls and the bookshelves and toys inside. His bedroom had been bare, with peeling wallpaper and a mattress on the floor.

It seemed like another person's life, it had become such a faded memory. Yet he knew the scars were still there. He'd been afraid of those scars, afraid they might prevent him from trusting anyone ever again.

But since he'd met Regan, the scars didn't seem so important. They were just reminders of his past, of a childhood that had offered him few opportunities. And yet in spite of that, he and his brothers had managed to not only survive but excel. He, for one, was ready to put the past in the past.

His parents might not have offered a good example of love and marriage. But that didn't mean he couldn't recognize real love. There was something about Regan that drew them together, beyond the physical attraction. Was that love?

Somehow, he'd have to trust that he'd know. There were plenty of other people in the world who'd had crappy childhoods and had found happiness. Why couldn't he be one of them?

He smiled to himself as he pulled away from the curb. There was one more place he wanted to see.

Winding through the narrow streets, he found the alley and slowed the truck, searching for the right garage.

Jamie recognized the window at the peak, but as he approached, he realized the door to the garage was open. As he passed by, he saw a familiar car inside, an old Thunderbird convertible, with a turquoise paint job. After nearly twenty years, the same guy was still working out of the same garage.

Jamie pulled the truck over to the side of the alley and turned off the ignition. The man looked up from beneath the hood of a battered Chevy Impala next to the convertible and watched as Jamie approached.

"That's a nice looking T-Bird," Jamie said, nodding to the sports car. "What is that, a '63 or '64?"

"It's a '63," the elderly man said.

"Nice. What ever happened to that little green MG you used to have?"

"Man, I sold that ten, twelve years ago. How do you know I used to own an MG?"

"I lived in the neighborhood many years ago," Jamie said. "In fact, I used to live in the loft of your garage.

Me and my two brothers spent about six months living up there until Social Services caught up with us."

"So you're the ones," he said, chuckling softly. "I found your stuff about the same time I sold the MG. At first I was pretty irritated, but then I realized you hadn't stolen anything. No harm, no foul. I figured if you were living in the loft of an old garage, then things probably weren't great at home."

Jamie shrugged. "We managed. I have to say, we did appreciate the warm place to sleep at night, so thank you." He held out his hand. "My name's Quinn. Jamie Quinn."

"Arthur Conrad," the old man said, grabbing Jamie's hand. "Most everyone calls me Arty."

"Nice to finally meet you, Arty."

"I can't believe I never caught you up there."

"Well, we knew you worked on your cars on the weekends, so we made ourselves scarce until late at night. We did get stuck upstairs a couple times when you came into the garage unexpectedly, but we were quiet until you left."

Arty chuckled, shaking his head. "Funny thing. When I found your stuff, I thought I might see you again so I kept it. You had quite a collection of comic books."

"You kept those?"

Arty stepped into the garage and walked back to a set of cluttered shelves. He rummaged through a series of boxes, then pulled a battered shoebox from its place. "Here it is."

He set the box on his workbench and motioned Jamie inside. The moment Jamie opened the box, memories of his childhood came flooding back. He pulled out a Rubik's Cube and an old handheld video game. There was a deck of cards and some poker chips. And a stack of comic books. But when he pulled out an old photo, Jamie realized what a treasure Arty had kept for him.

The picture was of Jamie and his brothers standing in front of a Christmas tree at the after-school program that he and his brothers had attended. They were all dressed in a ragtag mix of hockey gear, clutching battered sticks and grinning at the camera.

"Look at this," he murmured. "I don't think we have a single photo from our childhood. God, we were so young. We seem happy in this picture." Jamie put the photo back in the box and set the cover on top. "Thanks for keeping this stuff. It means a lot."

"No problem," Arty said. "I'm glad to hear that you boys are okay. After I found that stuff, I couldn't help but be a little curious. Now I know."

Jamie shook his hand again, tucked the shoe box under his arm and walked back to the truck. He gave Arty a wave as he drove away, pondering the strange set of circumstances that had brought them together today. Why had he felt it necessary to revisit the past? He seemed to be doing a lot of that lately—contemplating the choices he'd made, questioning what the future would hold. Wondering if he could have more than he'd first assumed. Like a wife and a family of his own.

Maybe he just needed a reality check. Tristan was always good for that. The middle brother of the three Quinns was the most gregarious, the kind of guy who made friends easily, especially those of the female sex.

Jamie wasn't sure how much to tell Tristan about his recent musings. Though Tristan had had a lot of women in his life, he'd never mentioned to Jamie that he had any intention of settling down.

O'Malley's Pub, a small neighborhood tavern, was quiet when Jamie pulled up. It wasn't four o'clock yet, so most of the patrons were probably still at work. He expected to wait for Tristan's arrival, but when he got inside he found his brother sitting at the end of the bar nursing a pint of beer.

"Hey, brother," Jamie called as he strolled through the taproom. "You're early."

"I've had a long day," Tristan said.

His brother was a lawyer, working for a prominent Twin Cities firm in the area of real estate law. Jamie had thought about asking Tris to handle the paperwork for his deal with Ceci. But he hadn't yet told his brothers about his new business venture and he expected that when he did, their opinions might not be supportive. After all, he'd sold his condo and invested every last penny of his savings and retirement fund in order to get the business off the ground. They'd all lived with nothing for too long not to be wary of putting so much at risk.

Jamie slid onto a stool next to Tristan and ordered a beer, then grabbed the bowl of peanuts nearby and popped a few in his mouth. "I have something to show you. You're going to love this."

"What is it?"

"A blast from the past," Jamie said. "I was feeling nostalgic and decided to take a drive around our old neighborhood. Remember that garage we used to sleep in?"

"I try to forget that," Tristan said. "Why would you want to remember that period in our lives?"

Jamie shrugged. "I've just been doing a lot of thinking lately."

"That doesn't sound good," Tris said.

"But it is," Jamie said. "For a long time, my life was going in a certain direction. I thought I knew what I wanted and I was happy. And then I had an opportunity to change everything and I grabbed it. I didn't realize it, but the whole thing started in that garage, with three homeless kids."

"I don't get it," Tris said.

"I'll explain it more one day when the whole thing is a huge success. But in the meantime I have something to show you. The same guy who owned the garage when we were kids was still there. We had a nice chat and he gave me a box of the things that we left behind." Jamie reached inside his jacket pocket and pulled out the photo, tossing it down on the bar in front of Tristan. "That was in the box."

A slow grin spread across Tristan's face as he stared at the photo. "Look at this," he murmured, staring more closely at the picture. "Where was this taken?"

"At the Boys and Girls Club. Remember it had that outdoor rink we used to play on? Look how skinny you were," Jamie said.

"Look how short you were," Tris countered.

"Sometimes I can't believe we made it through and

came out so well. There were so many ways our lives could've gone wrong, and yet they didn't."

"We had each other and our grandmother," Tristan said. "That made all the difference. We didn't need anyone else."

"And what about now? Do you ever feel like you need someone now?"

"What? Like a friend?"

"Yeah, maybe. Or a girlfriend. Maybe a fiancée. Or a wife. Do you ever wonder about that?"

Tristan considered the question for a long time before he replied. "Yeah, as a matter of fact, I have been wondering about that a lot lately."

"Have you met someone?" Jamie asked.

"I have been dating this one woman. Not exactly dating but… What about you?"

Jamie considered his options. He could tell Tristan about Regan. His brother might offer him some good advice. Or he'd spend the rest of the night teasing Jamie about being a sappy romantic.

In the end, he decided to wait to say anything to his brothers about Regan. After all, he wasn't sure what Regan meant to him. He'd met her less than a month ago and they'd agreed that there would be nothing romantic between them. In a few weeks, it would probably be all over and he'd have nothing further to say. So why bring it up now?

But over the last few days, Jamie had begun to feel as if his life was shifting beneath him. He'd thought his feet were planted firmly on the ground, but now he was stumbling and searching, trying to figure out the past and the present and the future all at once. Who the hell was he? And what did he want from life?

Jamie reached out for his beer and took a long sip. "Have you ever gotten the feeling that your life is about to change? As if something big is coming but you don't know what it is?"

"Yeah," Tristan said. "I've been feeling a lot of that lately."

"So what do you do about it?"

Tristan shrugged. "Right now, I've just been hanging on tight and waiting for the ride to slow down."

"Trust me," Regan said. "She is absolutely of sound mind and body. And she's determined to do this."

Her father had called twice and now she was on the phone with her aunt, Ceci's eldest daughter. "A quarter million dollars?"

"I talked with the financial advisor and he supports her decision," Regan said. "He said she has plenty to live on. Even if she lost this investment, she'd still be fine. I ripped the first check up, but she had them cut another check."

"She'd be fine? What about us?" Aunt Pauline asked. "That money is supposed to go to her children. Not to some silly scheme to house the homeless. On top of that, I got a call from Sissy Jorgenson. She told me that she and Mother had lunch the other day and your grandmother was trying to get Sissy to invest, too, so this man could buy more houses for the homeless. I can't imagine what's going to happen if she starts shopping this ridiculous idea around town. Asking all the most important families for money, like some crazy beggar. It would be…humiliating."

"I'll talk to her," Regan promised.

"You had better. That's your job, Regan. You're the one who is supposed to be watching over her. If you can't handle her, then we'll have to find someone else."

"No, I can—handle her," Regan said, barely able to say the words. Her grandmother didn't require handling. In Regan's opinion, she didn't need anyone to tell her what to do or how to do it. Though she was in her midseventies, Celia Macintosh was fully capable of running her own life.

"Perhaps we should call a family meeting," Pauline said.

"That won't be necessary. I'll talk to her today, I promise."

Regan hung up the phone and slipped it into her pocket. Then she walked to the door and stepped out onto the rear deck. It was a perfect fall day, warm and breezy, with white clouds blowing across the bright blue sky.

Jamie had spent the previous night in the city. He'd had meetings with his partners over Ceci's offer and he had to finalize the plans for the cabin. He was due to start building on Monday. If the weather held, he could be finished in as little as a week.

She drew a ragged breath. Finished. That meant he'd be heading back to his life in the city. She'd considered praying for bad weather, just to keep him around a little longer, but then she chided herself for her selfishness. He was desperate to finish the project in time for their investors meetings. As his friend, she ought to support that.

His friend. That was the most that Regan could claim to be. She couldn't be his girlfriend because they'd never really dated. They were lovers, but there were so many different variables there. They were lovers who weren't in love. They were lovers with no future plans. No strings attached. Nothing but meaningless sex to look forward to.

Was it really meaningless? It was hard to think about the intimacy they shared without believing that it must mean something. There was a connection, the genesis of a relationship, that Regan couldn't deny. But she couldn't let it go deeper than that.

Regan's phone rang again and she cursed softly. She'd heard from four of Ceci's seven children and expected the remaining three to call and voice their displeasure. But to Regan's surprise, Jamie's number came up on the screen.

"Hello," she said.

"Hey, there. Where are you?"

"Where are *you*?" Regan asked.

"I'm standing in the middle of Ceci's kitchen and you're not here."

"I'm out on the deck," she said.

A few moments later, he appeared at the door, the phone still to his ear. "Hi," he said from the other side of the glass. His smile was so sweet, so boyish, that she couldn't help but feel better.

"Hi. I'm glad you're back."

"You are?"

Regan nodded.

"I'm glad to be back," Jamie said. He opened the door and stepped outside, then slowly crossed the deck to where she stood. "God, you are beautiful."

Regan felt her cheeks warm. Did he really believe that? Or was it just something he said to women to charm them? "I always look better in sunny weather."

"I think you'd look good in any kind of weather," he said.

"Can I hang up now?" Regan asked. "There's this guy I really have to kiss."

"Okay, bye," Jamie said. He shoved his phone in his jacket pocket and waited, his gaze fixed on hers.

Regan smiled. "I'll be right back," she teased.

"Where are you going?"

"To kiss that guy I told you about," she said.

He growled softly, then yanked her into his arms and kissed her. The moment their tongues met, Regan relaxed in his arms, his taste like a drug that soothed her nerves. All the stress of dealing with her family seemed to dissolve as her mind focused on his kiss.

He drew back and gazed down into her face. "I've missed you," he said, brushing her windblown hair out of her eyes.

"And I missed you," Regan replied. She took his hand and pulled him along to the steps that led to the lake. The sun hung close to the horizon and it promised to be a beautiful sunset.

"Are you sure we should get near the water? I'm not wearing a life jacket."

"The only way you're going in is if I push you," Regan said. "And I promise not to do that."

They walked to the end of the dock and sat down in the waning light. Jamie slipped his arm around her shoulders and pulled her close. She nuzzled her face into his shoulder and smiled. "Did you get Ceci's papers filed?"

"Yes—signed, sealed and delivered. We're going to start building on Monday. The modules will be dropped off on the weekend. My partner is bringing them up by truck."

"And in a week you'll be finished?"

"That's the plan," Jamie said.

They stared out at the western shore of the lake, neither one of them ready to ask the next question. What happened to them after the cottage was finished?

"It's probably for the best," Regan said. "I've been fielding phone calls from my parents and my aunts and uncles about Nana's investment in your company. They aren't happy."

Jamie sighed. "Yeah, I wondered if that was going to happen. It's a lot to invest in a start-up."

"They want me to convince her not to go ahead with it," Regan said. "And to make matters worse, Ceci has been soliciting money from other people for your company. I don't really know why she's doing this, but I think it might have something to do with me."

"You?"

Regan nodded. Why not tell him the truth? They hadn't made any promises to each other. And if he was really a gentleman, he might refuse to take the extra money if there was a chance Ceci had done it in an attempt to buy a husband for her favorite granddaughter.

"I'm afraid she's making the investment because of me."

Jamie frowned. "How so?"

"I think she's trying to buy me a husband." She waited for the statement to sink in. But Jamie seemed confused. "She's trying to buy you—for me."

He drew back. "That's a little crazy."

"I know. I don't care how you explain it to your partners and how you approach it with Ceci, but it's no reason to spend a quarter million dollars."

He reached out and took her hand. "How much would it take?"

"Take?"

"To get you to fall in love and marry me?"

She laughed, but the serious expression on Jamie's face remained unchanged. "Don't kid around about this. It's humiliating enough as it is."

"What if I want to change the terms of our relationship? What if I want to fall in love? How would we do that? What would it take?"

"Nothing has to change. This is my fault. I encouraged her to get back out in the world," Regan said. "She just went a bit overboard."

"I'll refuse to take the money," he said. "My partners will kill me, but I'll handle them. Just answer my question."

Regan shook her head. "I don't have an answer. It's a ridiculous question."

"I know you feel something for me. I can see it in

your eyes when we make love. I can hear it in your laugh. We care about each other. So what if it went further?"

"This conversation is over," she said, rising. "But if you really need a figure, then I'll say…three million. That's what it would take for me to fall in love with you."

She turned on her heel and strode down the dock. Jamie called her name, and when she didn't answer she heard him start to follow her. When he caught up, he grabbed her hand, but she snatched it away. "If you're not careful, I'll push you in."

"I'll jump in if you promise to warm me up."

"Are you always such a pain in the ass?"

"Fine, I'll leave the question of us for now. There is something else I need to ask you."

"Five million," she said. "I'm changing my answer to five million."

"I'm supposed to photograph the build process for the investors and later for publicity purposes, but I'm starting to think that it will take too much time away from the actual construction. So I was hoping I could hire you. You're still going to be in town and I need lots of photos."

"My specialty is photographing people, not buildings," she said. "I have an assistant that I work with who could do the job."

"No," he said. "It would have to be you."

"It's going to be cold. And I'll have to be out there from sunup to sunset. And the lighting will be horrible. And how can I make photos of walls and nails and wood interesting?"

"I don't expect them to be interesting," he said. "And you might as well admit it—you're going to be out on the site, anyway. You're too damn nosy to keep away." He bent close and brushed a kiss across her lips. "And I mean that in the best sense of the word."

"Nosy? Even in the best sense that's not much of a compliment."

"Okay, *curious* would probably be a better word. Or *inquisitive.* Or *lovely.*" Jamie nodded. "Yes, that's exactly the word I was looking for. You are lovely."

"All right. I'll take your photos. And I won't even charge you. But you're going to have to do one thing for me."

"Anything," he said.

"You need to move out of the lodge into the guest cottage. Ceci had the furnace fixed and I cleaned up my stuff, so it's all ready for you."

"And you?" he said. "Will you stay there with me?"

"I don't know," she said, shrugging. "Maybe... I just don't want Ceci to get any ideas."

"You think she suspects we've been seeing each other?" he asked.

"After the way we showed up in the kitchen the other day, how could she not? But she might have read more into our relationship than there is. She can get these ideas in her head. She just wants me to be happy and she believes she can make it happen for me. She can't help herself sometimes. And she likes you, which makes it worse."

"Just consider staying with me, okay?"

Regan only smiled, but in truth, she wasn't sure she should continue to spend her nights with him. She'd hardly slept at all last night because she'd been tossing and turning and thinking about how much she needed Jamie in her bed. The sooner she got used to sleeping alone again, the better.

7

"THAT'S A LOT of stuff."

Jamie glanced over at Regan. She had a keen knack for speaking the truth and that was never more evident than now. He and his partners had just finished unloading the truck. Each of the three modules came on two pallets, easily moved by a forklift that Sam had rented.

"It looks like a lot of pieces now," Jamie said, "but it will come together really fast."

Regan held her camera and snapped a picture of his face, then showed him the view screen. "Caption—what have I gotten myself into?"

"All right," Jamie said. "I'll admit, it's a little daunting. But I didn't expect it to be easy."

"Maybe you should hire a construction contractor to put it together and you can just supervise."

Jamie shook his head. "The whole point is to show that an average volunteer could put one of these together."

"Just one volunteer?" Regan said. "You have four people." She looked through the viewfinder and focused on him again. "Why don't you stand next to the pile? Then we can get a sense of the scale."

"I don't think it's necessary to get pictures of this phase of the job. I've got a couple of days until Construction Eve. I'll figure out how to do it myself." He'd watched a module be put together at the factory and it had seemed so simple and straightforward. Now, he was beginning to have his doubts.

Jamie reached in his pocket and grabbed the materials list. There were a few specific items he had yet to buy from the local hardware store. Once he completed that task, he'd be ready to start building. "I have to go into town," he said. "You want to come with me?"

"Sure," Regan said. "I have to meet a wedding planner at the studio in an hour, but it won't take me long. We can grab a quick lunch and then you can get your shopping done"

Jamie grinned. "Are you asking me out on a date?"

Her smile faded and Jamie knew that he'd pushed her too far. What was it with him? Why couldn't he just accept their relationship on her terms and enjoy it? Lately, he'd been constantly trying to renegotiate with her.

"Sorry," he murmured.

"No, it's all right," she said. "You were just joking."

"Or maybe I wasn't?" he countered.

"If a grilled cheese sandwich and a chocolate malt at the local diner constitutes a date, then yes, I'm asking you on a date."

Jamie threw his arm around her shoulders. "My day is getting better by the minute. A date!"

She jabbed him in the ribs with her elbow and he stumbled dramatically, trying to tease her into a smile. Jamie had to wonder how much longer that would work. He'd tried every way he knew how to get her to see what was happening between them, but she refused to recognize what was obvious to him.

He was in love with her. And she was falling in love with him.

They said goodbye to his partners and walked back up to the road, where Jamie had left his truck. He helped Regan inside, then jogged around to the driver's side. He started the truck and headed into town.

The road was damp from a morning rain and brightly colored leaves clung to the pavement, making it slippery in some spots. The weather had stayed relatively warm and the forecast predicted more of the same. Jamie was grateful; building the cottage in the rain would be miserable.

"Where would you like to go for lunch?" he asked.

"Lakeview Café would be good. Have you been there?"

"A couple times when I first came up here," Jamie said. He reached over and grabbed her hand, then brought it to his lips to kiss her wrist. "Our first date."

"We're having lunch," she said. "Don't make such a big deal of it. I don't want you to develop expectations."

"Is that why you hate romantic relationships? Because of expectations?"

"When you expect too much, you'll only be disappointed."

"And what if you don't expect anything at all?" Jamie asked.

"Then you'll always be happy with what you have."

She stared out at the road ahead and a long silence grew between them. He wanted to shake her, to make her see how much she was missing with such a pessimistic attitude.

There were moments—tiny moments—when he'd catch her looking at him, or when she'd say something without thinking, or when she'd touch him, and he knew she was feeling something deeper for him.

Their physical relationship had changed, as well. The sex was just as powerful, but it was also sweet and tender, tinged with pure affection.

"After lunch, I'll probably be tired and need a nap."

"You always want to take a nap and then we never actually sleep," Regan said.

"You're right. What's that all about?"

"You know exactly what it's about," she said with a laugh, pointing to his crotch.

Now that she had brought it up, he did want to discuss their sleeping arrangements. Since her grandmother had returned, Jamie had been living in the guest cottage. Though it provided plenty of privacy for the two of them, Regan refused to spend the entire night in his bed. She stayed until just before the sun came up, then threw her boots on and sneaked back to the house. "Why won't you spend the whole night with me? Your grandmother doesn't seem to mind that we're spending time together."

"You have no idea what's going on in Ceci's mind," Regan warned him. "I'd rather be there when she wakes up in the morning than have her speculating about what's going on between us. As far as she'd concerned, people who sleep together are supposed to get married."

"But you're acting like there's nothing going on between us *at all*," Jamie protested. "And that's not true."

She stared out the passenger side window, watching as the truck moved through the outskirts of Pickett Lake. "Can we talk about this later? At home?"

Jamie nodded. "There are probably a lot of things we ought to discuss," he murmured. "By the way, if I ever meet this Jake guy, I'm going to beat the ever-loving crap out of him. He really hurt you."

He pulled the truck up in front of the café and parked it. Regan hopped out and joined him on the sidewalk. When they entered the front door, she called a greeting to the owner, who stood near the cash register, folding napkins. Regan seemed to know most of the waitresses, as well, and when a woman whose name tag read Valerie approached with a pair of menus, Regan chatted for a moment with her about her two children.

Jamie opened the menu. "What are you going to have? Order anything. My treat."

"So this is one of those dates that isn't dutch," she said. "Must be serious."

He reached under the table and gave her thigh a squeeze. "Of course it's serious. Dating is serious business."

He gave her a silly look to make her laugh. Then he began to put their table in perfect order, lining up all the silverware and squaring up the paper place mats. It was something he'd caught her doing, and now he found it amusing to mimic her behavior.

"Very funny," she said.

"I should start carrying a ruler so I can get it perfect."

"So I'm fussy," she said. "You shouldn't make fun of a person's mental infirmities."

"I love your mental infirmities," he said. "No one appreciates them more than I do. I like how you always fold the end of the toilet paper before you leave the bathroom."

"You noticed that?"

"At first I thought it might be elves, but then I figured out it was you. And the way you keep the flavors of ice cream in alphabetical order in the freezer."

"That's so I can find what I want faster." She reached out and took his hand, bringing it to her lips. "I'm sorry for being such a bitch," Regan murmured. "And for raining all over our first date. I guess I woke up on the wrong side of the bed today."

"That's because you didn't wake up with me," Jamie said. "That makes all the difference. Sleeping with me has restorative powers."

A laugh bubbled from her throat. "Is that what you're calling it? Restorative powers. Hmm…"

Jamie congratulated himself on putting Regan in a better mood. Sometimes all he needed to feel better was the sound of her laugh, and he'd learned how to deliberately induce it. He loved it when he got her laughing and she couldn't stop.

Jamie smiled as she peered at him over the edge of the menu, trying to calm herself. But then, in a heartbeat, her laughter stopped and her eyes went wide. Jamie turned to see a young couple entering the café.

"Oh, God," she said, lowering her head.

"What?"

"It's him," she said in a strangled tone. "You said it and now he's here."

"Regan?" the other man said.

Jamie slowly stood. Regan did the same. Her hands were clutched in front of her and all the blood had drained out of her face. "Hello, Jake. What are you doing here?"

Jamie glanced back and forth between the two of them. So this was Jake Lindstrom—the man who'd left Regan at the altar. The man who'd broken her heart and her spirit and her trust. He felt his hand clench into a fist. He ought to flatten the guy right here and now.

But then Jamie rethought his first impulse. He ought to thank him. If he hadn't left Regan standing at the altar, then Jamie never would have had the chance to fall for her.

"We came home for the fall colors," Jake explained. "Regan, this is my fiancée, Kelly. Kelly, this is my old friend Regan Macintosh."

Kelly held out her hand, and when Regan didn't take it, Jamie reached out. "Hi, I'm Jamie. I'm Regan's fiancé. It's a pleasure to meet you." He shook Jake's hand.

"She's told me so much about you. All about how you were...old friends."

"A pleasure," Regan repeated, taking Kelly's hand. She avoided touching Jake.

Jamie slipped his arm around Regan's waist. She stood silently, listening as he attempted to make stilted conversation with the couple—the best places to see the color, the weather, the temperature of the lake.

Finally, the pair excused themselves to fetch a couple cups of coffee. "Just smile and nod," Jamie whispered. "And sit down. They'll be gone in a minute."

She did as she was told, and when Jake and his fiancée finally left, Jamie gave her back a pat and she released a tightly held breath.

"Please tell me I didn't sound like an idiot," Regan said.

"You didn't say much, so I guess you didn't sound like an idiot."

Regan pressed her hand to her chest and winced. "He's engaged? My mom said he was still single— Wait." She turned to him. "We're engaged?"

"I didn't know what to say. I figured you might be okay with the lie. People always fake engagements when they run into exes in the movies."

"I can't believe he just walked up to me and introduced his fiancée. After everything he did to me. I had all these plans of what I'd say to him the next time I saw him, and then, when I had the opportunity, I couldn't even speak." She groaned and covered her face with her hands.

"Are you still in love with him?" Jamie asked.

He didn't want to hear the answer to his question, though he feared her reaction was answer enough. But Jamie couldn't help but hope that he was wrong.

"No!" Regan cried. "Of course I don't love him. I—I guess I just hoped he might have suffered a little more, like the way he made me suffer. But she's beautiful and smart and they look like the perfect couple." She moaned again. "Why couldn't he have ended up with some awful bleach-blond harpy with bad teeth and horrible fashion sense?"

"You're smart," Jamie said. "And beautiful. There's no reason for you to be jealous of her."

Regan looked up. "I can't eat now. My stomach hurts and I feel like throwing up. I'm just going to walk over to my studio while you hit the hardware store. Pick me up when you're done."

"Regan, come on. Don't let him get to you. It's not a big deal."

She bent close and pressed a kiss to his cheek. "Thank you," she murmured. "For the fiancé thing. I really appreciate it."

Shaking his head Jamie watched her walk out. There were moments when he felt as if he knew her so well that he could predict her every reaction and response. And then there were times like this, when he realized he didn't know Regan Macintosh at all. Yet it didn't seem to matter to him. He was falling in love with her and there was nothing he could do about it.

REGAN STOOD IN the center of her gallery space, her eyes closed, her head tipped back. She was exhausted, as if the last bit of energy had been sucked from her body, leaving her immobile and unable to feel.

What the heck was wrong with her? Over the years since her botched wedding, Regan thought she'd grown stronger, at least a little bit. But no, all it had taken was one look and she'd crumpled into a hot mess. Jake had found happiness and she hadn't. He was moving on with his life, building a family and finally making the dream they'd dreamed happen.

And what had she done? The one man who had caught her attention was just a friend. She'd insisted on keeping him at arm's length, convincing herself that they couldn't possibly have a future together. And it was just as well. If she was still this affected by Jake, what kind of mess would she be if she ran into Jamie one day with his beautiful fiancée?

She walked over to the studio phone and listened to her voice mail, then flipped on the computer and checked her email. Regan had four new requests for her wedding services and two for family holiday photos. And the wedding planner she'd arranged to meet in a half hour had canceled. She checked the dates from the prospective clients against her calendar. Only one wedding was a possibility, but she could fit in the two family shoots after Sedona and before Christmas.

She walked back to the storage room and grabbed a camera bag, loading it with lenses and filters for the cottage shoot. She decided to grab a traditional camera, as well, adding both black-and-white and color film to the bag. Then she pulled out the small tent that she used to store her equipment in the case of rain.

As she pulled the tent bag off the bottom shelf, she noticed a large white box covered with a thin coat of dust. Regan reached out for it, then snatched her hand away. What good would it do to look at it now? Her day had already gone to hell once. Why drive it right back there again?

And yet she couldn't help herself. She needed to remember how it had felt. She could never move past her complicated feelings about love and romance if she never allowed herself to think about the reason they were complicated. It was time to tear off the bandage and look at the wound.

She dragged the box out into the studio, then set it on top of a table. Drawing a deep breath, Regan removed the cover and pushed back the tissue paper. She sighed as her fingertips dropped to the white silk.

She moved the veil aside and grabbed the shoulders of the gown, then pulled the dress out of the box. The crinoline beneath the cream-colored silk rustled and she smiled at the memories that the sound brought back. Before Jake walked out on her, she'd tried to remember every moment of the day, knowing she'd want to relive it in later years. But now she realized she hadn't needed to make the effort. She would never forget a moment of that day.

It was a beautiful dress. The princess lines of the bodice had been fitted to her body like a second skin and the wide skirt fell in a graceful drape. But it was the neckline that made the dress, a wide portrait with off-the-shoulder cap sleeves. There were no beads on the dress, no sparkly crystals. Just yards and yards of luxurious silk.

She picked the gown up and held it against her, then crossed to the full-length mirror against the wall. She'd kept the dress, thinking that she'd wear it when she and Jake finally did get married—after he realized his mistake and came begging for her forgiveness.

"I guess that's not going to happen," she muttered. Not that she really wanted to marry Jake now.

She hummed a tune to herself as she swayed in front of the mirror. Would it still fit? She tossed it over a nearby chair and quickly removed her clothes. Then she unzipped the dress and stepped into it, slipping her arms through the cap sleeves. Reaching behind her, she drew the zipper up until it stopped in the center of her back.

It still fit perfectly. But as she stared at herself in the mirror, Regan barely recognized herself. She'd once thought the dress was the most beautiful gown in the world, but now she looked like some princess wannabe. Her younger self had had all the wonderful fantasies of a bride and none of the realities of what being a wife would require.

"I should have thanked him," Regan murmured. "I may have been ready for a wedding, but I wasn't ready to be married." Jake must have sensed that. Or maybe he hadn't been ready, either. All these years she'd been so angry with him, and all along, he'd saved her life.

"I guess I was right to be worried about you."

Regan spun around to see Jamie standing in the archway between the gallery and the studio. He watched her, a wary look in his eye.

"Oh, God. This isn't what it seems like," she declared.

"I have no idea what it seems like," Jamie said. "Maybe you could explain."

"The dress—I've been saving it. I thought that I'd wear it again. It was so perfect and it took me forever to find it. It's kind of a thing with brides when you put the dress on. It's like it magically transforms you into a princess. I came across the box today and I just wanted to see if I still felt that way."

"Like a princess?"

Regan nodded. "It probably sounds silly to you, but trust me. When you're a girl, you dream about your wedding gown from the moment you start noticing boys."

"That's kind of a frightening thought," Jamie said.

She walked across the studio and sat down on the antique chaise. "I guess that's why it's kind of a closely held secret."

"What other secrets do women keep from men?"

"Oh, there are probably hundreds," Regan admitted.

"Maybe someone ought to put them down in a book," Jamie suggested.

She shrugged and flopped back on the chaise, throwing her arm over her eyes. "You know what's really strange?" she asked.

"There's something stranger than seeing you in a wedding gown?"

"I'm not really embarrassed. I should be, but if anyone is going to see me like this, I'm glad it was you. You'll at least try to understand."

Jamie crossed the room and sat down on the chaise beside her. It was only then that she noticed the small bag he carried. "What's in there?"

"A chocolate malt. Guys have secrets, too, and this is one of them. We believe that chocolate or ice cream can cheer up even the most despondent female."

"That's a good rule," she said, taking the bag from his hand. Regan pulled out the paper cup and pushed the straw into the top, then took a long sip. "Very good rule. Thank you."

He smiled at her. "You're easy to please."

"Did you get your shopping done?"

He held his hand out and she gave him the malt. Jamie took a sip, then passed it back to her. "Yep. I got everything on the list. Except the chain saw. I still haven't decided whether to get that. I've never operated a chainsaw. I'm not comfortable taking down those maple trees with it by myself. I'll probably kill myself. I'd either cut off an arm or leg or drop a tree on my head."

"We can't have that. I could help you out with the chainsaw," Regan said.

"Please don't tell me you can operate one."

She shook her head. "No. And I can't cut down trees, either. But I know the person to call."

"And here I thought I was going to learn another one of those ladies-only secrets—you all know how to use power tools."

"Not all of us, sorry to say."

He pulled her closer and kissed the top of her head.

"Are you going to spend the rest of the day in that gown?"

She nodded. "Would you be upset if I did?"

"No, you look very pretty. But you also look pretty without clothes." Jamie stood up and held out his hand. "Come on. I'll take you back to the cottage. We'll pick up a pizza on the way home."

He pulled her to her feet and then dragged her into his embrace, giving her a long, lazy kiss. When he finally stepped back, Jamie shook his head. "I'm kissing the bride," he said. "It should be freaking me out, but it's not so bad."

He helped her into her jacket, then picked up her clothes, which she'd scattered on the floor. "We probably should have gotten a few photos while we were here," he suggested. "Just as a memento of this very strange day."

"There are some stories that pictures will never convey."

Regan watched as he buttoned the front of her jacket, covering the bodice of the huge white gown.

There was no question about it anymore. She was falling in love with Jamie Quinn. How was she possibly going to protect herself from being devastated when he left her, too?

"If you expect me to carry you over the threshold," he said, "you're going to have to give me some serious quid pro quo."

She laughed in spite of her dark thoughts. She'd worry about the end of their relationship later. For now, she'd enjoy the time they had. "I'm sure we can come to some agreement."

"EDDIE RAYNER WILL be here on Saturday morning," Regan said. Still clad in the white silk gown, she sipped at a cup of hot cocoa as she stood next to the fire. "He'll clear the trees for you and you will not lose any limbs on this job."

Jamie observed her from the sofa as she paced back and forth in front of the fireplace. "Are you ever going to take that dress off?" he asked.

"I'm waiting for you to take it off," she said. "Besides, I really should get some wear out of it. It cost seventeen thousand dollars."

Jamie gasped. "Seventeen thousand? That's crazy."

"Weddings are a crazy business," she said with a shrug.

"So if you had to do it all over again, would you do the big dress and the fancy ceremony?"

She took another sip of her cocoa and Jamie watched as she licked her upper lip. "I don't think so," she said. "Now it just seems like a lot of sugarcoating for a ceremony that should be about love and commitment. There would have to be lots of flowers and candles, though. But I'd be just as comfortable in jeans and bare feet, standing on a beach somewhere. Maybe right out there," she said, looking out at the lake.

He pulled her down next to him and lifted the hem of the gown. "You do have beautiful feet," he murmured. Jamie wrapped his fingers around her ankle and drew her foot up to place a kiss on her deep arch.

"Eddie asked if you could mark the trees you want him to take down," she said, watching Jamie with half-closed eyes. "He recommended tying scraps of fabric around the trunks. He'll cut up the trees and leave the firewood. He'll also get rid of all the brush."

"What's he going to charge? My budget is pretty tight."

"Don't worry. Ceci already convinced him of how important your cause is. He's agreed to do it pro bono."

"That's great. Ceci's becoming a real asset to the company," he said, laughing. Then he sobered. "I'm going to have to tell your grandmother about the maples," he said.

"I mentioned it to her and she didn't seem to have a problem with it," Regan said. "In fact, she said that she might not have time for syrup this spring, anyway. She and Cal are planning to take a cruise."

"That sounds serious," Jamie said. "They're moving awfully fast, don't you think?"

"I'm all right with it now," Regan said. "When you know it's right, you just know. She's been so lonely. She deserves this. And Cal is an old family friend. Everyone loves him. She couldn't have chosen better."

"You Macintosh girls make things so easy," Jamie said with a grin. He pushed the gown up farther and began to massage her bare calf. There were times when all he wanted to do was touch her, to make a concentrated study of her body. This was one of those moments, Jamie mused. Except her body seemed trapped beneath yards and yards of creamy silk.

"So what are your plans for the next few days?" she asked, watching him attend to her right foot.

"I have to dig twelve holes for the cottage footings,"

he said. "With a shovel and a pick. Three modules, four corners each. I figure it will take the entire day."

"I could help," Regan said.

Jamie shook his head. "I have to do as much as I can by myself. And my business partners are coming out to watch. And you need to take photos."

"We're all just going to sit around and watch you work?" Regan asked.

"I guess so," Jamie said.

In truth, he was looking forward to finally starting the project. He'd set a huge goal for himself, one that was probably impossible to achieve. But he relished the challenge.

He knew the basics of construction, and could hammer a nail and operate most power tools. But to do the project on his own, he'd have to get creative with other tasks. He just hoped that the weather held and he didn't injure himself.

Though it was difficult to imagine the project finished, Jamie knew it wouldn't take long. Building a traditional home on the lake could take a year or two, but their modules were made for quick and simple installation. There wouldn't be any long discussions about cabinet colors and faucet finishes.

"We're going to have to find a way to celebrate when the project is done," he said, searching for a way to keep her with him longer.

"We could throw a party. Ceci would love that. We could invite everyone in town. You might even sell a few more cottages."

"That's a good idea," Jamie said. "But it's not the

kind of celebration I was thinking about. I was thinking about us. Maybe taking a little vacation together. Maybe a cruise, like Cal and Ceci."

Regan frowned. "Aren't we always on vacation?"

"You know what I mean. We could get away. Lie on a beach somewhere and figure out what all this means."

"We don't need a beach to do that," Regan said.

"So your answer is no?"

She shook her head. "I'm not saying anything right now."

"I realize I agreed that this was just going to be a short-term thing, but I'd really like to continue to see you. We don't live that far from each other. And even when you're in Arizona for the winter, you could come home. And I could go there."

"We don't have to decide this now, do we?"

He shook his head. Jamie regretted bringing the subject up at all. It had created a tension between them that hadn't been there before. Was she really ready to end it when the cabin was finished? Had he misread the situation entirely?

"What do you want?" he asked.

"I'd like to get out of this dress, for a start," she said.

"I can help with that," Jamie offered.

After living in the main lodge for almost a week, he found the guest cottage a cozy change. It was only one large room that served as a bedroom, sitting room and compact kitchen. An entire wall of windows overlooked the lake. Unlike the main lodge, the cottage was at water level and nearer to the shore. Even with the windows closed, he could fall asleep to the sound of water lapping.

Regan stood up and turned her back to him. Jamie slowly worked the zipper down to her waist. He pressed a kiss to her shoulder, then trailed his lips along the same path. The scent of lavender filled his head and he wondered if he'd ever smell the fragrance without thinking of her.

"This is exactly how it should be," she murmured.

"What's that?"

"You removing this dress. When I step out of it, my past will be completely in the past. It's like I'm shedding my skin."

"A seventeen-thousand-dollar skin," he said.

He reached up and grabbed the edges of the sleeves, hooking his fingers around the fabric and pulling the bodice down over her arms and torso. Then he dragged the massive skirt over her hips, until it lay like a cloud around her feet.

Dressed in just her bra and panties, she stared down at the wedding gown, then kicked it aside. "Maybe we can use it for curtains in the new cabin."

"You look like a goddess," he said.

"A goddess who didn't get lunch," she said, rubbing her arms.

"Do you want me to make you something?"

Regan shook her head. "Why don't you build the fire up and I'll get a snack." She headed for the kitchen. She'd stayed in the cottage over the summer, but when the cooler weather of fall set in, the broken furnace had sent her back to her room in the main house. Luckily, the cottage was still stocked with some of her favorite snacks.

Regan grabbed a short bathrobe from a peg on the wall and slipped it over her arms. The pretty red silk fluttered out behind her as she walked. Jamie kept his eyes on her as she moved about the kitchen. He'd taken moments like this for granted, but after next week, they'd go back to their regular lives.

Regan had made it very clear from the start that she was interested in only a short-term relationship. And at the time, Jamie had agreed. But all that had changed. Even she would have to admit that they'd moved beyond the physical.

Yes, the time they spent in bed was still a considerable part of their day-to-day contact. But there were many moments in between that made him believe she might have changed her mind about the two of them. But his suggestion of a vacation had been met with indifference. If she were considering a future with him, she might have responded with a bit more enthusiasm.

Perhaps this was poetic justice, Jamie thought to himself. He'd mostly treated women like a temporary enjoyment in his life until this point. Now that he'd found one he wanted to stick around, she didn't share his affections.

"What are you making?"

"S'mores," she said. "Look on the rack with the fireplace tools. There should be two campfire forks hanging on it."

He grabbed the forks and sat down in front of the fire. The flames crackled at the new wood he'd just added, but below the grate, embers pulsed with a red-hot heat.

Regan joined him in front of the fire with a plate of graham crackers, chocolate chips and large marshmallows. "Have you ever had a s'more?" she asked, kneeling beside him.

"My brothers and I used to live on s'mores," he said. "We'd each be responsible for one item. You could usually find all three at a well-stocked mini-mart. They usually let me lift the crackers. The shelf stockers in the store usually kept a close eye on the candy shelves when kids were hanging around, so it could be hard to sneak something out under your jacket."

"You shoplifted the ingredients?"

He shrugged. "Only when we didn't have a choice," he said. "Finding food was always a problem. We had a free lunch at school, but in the summers, we were on our own. And of course, we preferred s'mores to anything else. We'd wrap them up in foil and stick them in an old toaster my brother found."

She sat back on her heels and shook her head. "There are times when I really think I know you. And then you tell me something new and it completely changes my understanding of you."

"Is that bad?" he asked.

She bent forward and touched her lips to his, then shook her head. "No. I want to know more."

"It's not always pretty," he warned.

"I understand. But it always amazes me that you were able to survive, and that you turned out to be such an extraordinary man."

"You like me, don't you?"

"I do," she said.

"Am I your boyfriend?"

"You're my friend and you're a boy, so, yes, you are my boyfriend."

Jamie slowly shook his head. "Seriously, Regan. Am I your boyfriend? I know we're lovers. But if you had been given the chance to introduce me to Jake, how would you have done it?"

"I'm not sure," she said. "And I don't want to think about it right now." Regan shoved the plate aside and crawled onto his lap, wrapping her arms around his neck. "Can't we just enjoy what we have and figure out how to label it later?"

Jamie sighed. They had another week together. Which meant he had another week to convince her that she couldn't put their relationship in a tidy little box and leave it behind. Another week to transform himself from a lover to a boyfriend. Another week.

It didn't seem like enough. But he had to trust that her feelings had been changing right along with his, only she was too afraid to admit it. If he could only find an antidote to her fear, he might have a chance to make it work.

"All right," she said, sighing dramatically. "If you want labels, I'll give you some labels." Regan leaned forward and kissed him. "Kiss," she murmured. "Lips. Tongue. Soft. Damp."

Jamie moaned as she drew him closer, deepening the contact until she'd wiped away his irritation and replaced it with need.

She untied her robe and shrugged out of it, then grabbed his hand, bringing it up to cover her breast.

"Breast," he murmured.

"Very good," Regan said.

He dragged the bra straps off her shoulders, then unhooked the back. The lacy garment fell away, revealing perfect mounds of flesh, tipped in pink. His lips drifted lower. "Nipple," he said, before bringing it to a peak with his tongue.

"You're a quick study," she said.

He laced his fingers through hers and gently pulled her down to the floor on top of him, her body stretched along the length of his. He was already hard, and as she shifted against him, currents of desire set his nerves on fire, until there was only one thing he truly needed.

Regan slipped to his side, then ran her hand down his chest. Deft fingers opened the button on his jeans and drew the zipper down. Jamie held his breath, waiting for that moment when her touch met his hard shaft.

"And this?" she said.

"There's all kinds of labels for that," he said, as she closed her fingers around him. Slowly, she began to stroke, her hand smoothing from the base to the tip and then back again. "How about we call it yours."

"Mine?" She glanced up at him, a satisfied grin curling her lips.

"Sure. You seem to be entirely in command of it these days, so I guess I should admit defeat and take it like a man."

She grabbed the waist of his jeans and gently tugged

them down. "I don't know about this. They don't allow pets at my apartment. And I have no idea what to feed it."

"Sure you do," he teased.

"Oh, I remember now." She reached between them and pulled aside her panties, then slowly guided him inside her. Jamie watched her face as she moved, sinking down on top of him one delicious inch at a time.

With her naked body open to his touch and gaze, he was already on the edge, yet his clothes created a barrier between them. They were joined in just one spot, and every nerve in his body seemed to be focused there.

"Condom," he murmured, realizing that they'd missed an important step.

"It's all right," she said. "I have that covered."

"You're a really good lover," he said with a grin.

"I am."

And someday she'd be much more, Jamie thought to himself. He'd find a way to make it happen, whether she was ready to surrender to the truth or not. They were meant to be together.

8

REGAN PEERED THROUGH her camera viewfinder, focusing the lens on Jamie's rain-soaked face. It was late afternoon and the light was nearly gone. He looked like he was in genuine pain and Regan wanted to cry for him.

This was all her fault. He'd spent the entire day trying to dig holes for the concrete footings that would support his house modules. But the land beneath his feet would not cooperate.

The shoreline north of the lodge was clear of trees, but now it was apparent why. The area was almost all solid rock. After a day of grueling labor, he'd almost finished four holes, chipping away at the rock bit by bit, using an air hammer that he'd rented in town. The rain had begun shortly after he'd measured everything out, marking each corner with stakes he'd pounded into the shallow topsoil that covered the rock.

Throughout the day, people had stopped by to check on his progress. Apparently, Jamie had made the mistake of explaining his construction schedule to Walt

Murphy at the hardware store, who decided to pass the information on to nearly everyone in Pickett Lake. The sight of a man building a cabin solo in just a week was too much for most of the retired men in town to miss.

Digging down forty-two inches into solid rock had left Jamie covered with mud from head to toe. Several of the men from town had offered to help, but Jamie had politely turned them down, insisting that he needed to do all the work himself.

Regan glanced out across the lake. The sun was setting and a bitter chill had set into the late afternoon air. The wind was picking up and she knew he was close to exhaustion.

She put her camera back in its case and tucked it beneath her arm. Then she trudged over to Jamie. He stared down into the hole, water dripping off the hood of his jacket and the tip of his nose.

She reached out and touched his cheek. He jerked and looked up at her, as if he hadn't noticed her approach.

"Come on," she said. "Time to call it a day."

He shook his head. "I have to get these done," he said. "These holes are going to need to dry out before I can pour the concrete, and that requires a day to cure before I can put the floor deck on. I actually thought I'd get the footings poured today."

"This is ridiculous," she said.

"Yes, but there's not much I can do about it."

Regan took a deep breath and swallowed back another flood of tears. "There's something that I can do about it. You can forget this crappy piece of shoreline and you can build on the point."

"But I thought you—"

"I've changed my mind. You're going to kill yourself trying to make this work. And we both know your model home will look much better on Maple Point. That's where I want it."

"We've already lost too much time," he said. "We'd have to clear more trees over there and I'd have to dig another four holes for the footings."

"We'll get Eddy back here in the morning. And for the footings, we'll use that posthole digger and it will be done by the end of the day. I'll help you," Regan said. "It's my fault we're in this mess, anyway."

He glanced back and forth between her face and the hole, then finally tossed the shovel aside and stepped away. "All right," he said. He wrapped his arms around her and pulled her into a fierce embrace.

When he cupped her face, his fingers were so cold she flinched. He'd discarded his gloves long ago. Regan grabbed one hand and tucked it in her jacket pocket, gently massaging his fingers to warm them.

"Are you hungry?" she asked. "I made some beef stew in the crockpot. It's Ceci's recipe. It's really good."

"I can't tell if I'm hungry," he said. "I think my whole body is frozen."

They walked along the water's edge, Regan helping Jamie when he stumbled. He turned toward the guest cabin, but Regan pulled him along. "Ceci is at a play with Cal," she said. "I'm going to put you in the steam shower to warm up while I get dinner ready."

When they reached the deck of the lodge, they slowly

climbed the steps, Jamie leaning on her as if his body were about to give out.

The moment they got to the back door, she began to strip the muddy clothes off his body, first his boots and socks, then his jeans and jacket, and finally his T-shirt, soaked with perspiration. She added her own boots to the pile, then grabbed the door.

"Come on, hurry up," she said, dragging him inside. She quickly shrugged out of her jacket and pulled him over to the fireplace. Then she grabbed a quilt from the back of the sofa and wrapped it around his nearly naked body.

Regan wrapped her arms around him and began to rub his back through the quilt. His hair continued to drip and she smoothed a strand out of his eyes. "You smell like a wet dog," she said. "And you kind of look like one, too."

"I should have started this project in the summer," he said.

"Oh, but then the mosquitoes would have carried you away," she said. "Spring and fall are always the best. Out of curiosity, why didn't you start earlier?"

"We needed the money from the sale of my condo to get the land," he said. "It just closed last month."

"And why does it have to be done by November 1?"

"We have a group of investors coming next week to see the product. We have one of the single modules built in the city. But we wanted to sell them on a multi-module design."

"And what if you don't finish?"

"I'm going to finish," he said.

"But what if you don't?"

He gave a shrug, wiping at his wet nose with the corner of the quilt. "Then I've failed."

Regan took his hand and drew him away from the fire. "Come on, I think you can make it up the stairs now."

She wrapped her arm around his waist and walked with him to the guest bedroom, then into the bathroom. She set the controls for the steam, then reached inside the shower to turn it on. When it was ready, she went back to get Jamie. "Stay in there for at least ten minutes. Then put on the sweatshirt and pants I left on the bed. I'll bring supper up here and you can eat in bed."

"You're not coming in with me?"

She gave him a gentle shove until he stood under the shower. "Don't forget to take your boxers off." Regan closed the glass door and walked out of the bathroom. She'd found the sweatshirt and fleece pants in the hodgepodge of clothes that her grandmother kept around for the family.

As for her own damp clothes, Regan hurried to her bedroom and stripped out of them, choosing a pair of flannel pajamas and wool socks to warm her cold limbs.

Before she went back downstairs, she peeked in the bathroom. Through the steamy glass door, she could see Jamie, naked, his hands braced on the marble wall as the water poured down his spine.

When she got to the kitchen, Regan set a tray on the counter and began to load it with food. Two bowls of piping hot stew, a rich mix of meat and vegetables. She cut up a baguette and spread the slices with butter before dropping them into a small basket. She finished with a couple bottles of beer and a huge glass of milk, not sure what he'd want to drink.

Her cell phone rang as she scooped up some pie for dessert. Regan picked it up from the counter and noticed a few missed calls from her grandmother's new cell. "Hi, Nana."

"Hello, darling. How are things going? Did Jamie spend the whole day out in the rain?"

"Yes, he did. But I talked him inside and he's warming up in the shower. I made your famous beef stew for dinner, so that should finish the job if the shower doesn't." She paused. "Nana, I decided to give him Maple Point for the cottage. The other piece of land is solid rock, and he can't build on that."

"Of course he can't. But you don't have to consult with me about the point. Maple Point is yours to give."

"Is it, Nana?"

"It's in my will, so I'd say you're the one who can make that decision."

"Did you make this mess on purpose?"

"Whatever do you mean?" she asked. "But I also called to let you know that we're going to stay in the city after the play. The rain is supposed to turn to sleet and the roads will get slippery."

"Where are you going to stay?"

"I'm sure we'll just get a hotel room," Ceci said.

"Nana! You naughty girl. I hope you're going to get separate rooms. We wouldn't want to harm your reputation."

"Darling, there comes a point where having a reputation is the only thing that an old lady like me can look forward to."

"You're not old, Nana. You're as young as you feel."

"Well, I must say, I feel like I'm about twenty-five."

Regan smiled. "That's wonderful. You and Cal have fun. We'll see you tomorrow."

She switched the phone off and slipped it into the pocket of her pajama pants, then finished her dessert preparations, adding a can of whipped cream to the tray. Carefully, she grabbed the handles and balanced the weight, then headed upstairs.

From the hall, she could hear that the water was off. But when she walked through the bedroom doorway, she stopped short. Jamie was lying across the bed, a towel wrapped around his waist, his arms thrown out to the sides.

"Jamie?"

He didn't move and she noticed his breathing was deep and even. She set the tray on the dresser, then crossed to the bed, sat beside him and shook his shoulder. "Hey, Jamie."

He pushed up on his elbows and looked around, his eyes half-closed. "Yeah?"

Regan stood, then got him to his feet. She pulled the covers back, grabbed the towel from his waist and gently pushed him into the bed. He always slept naked, anyway. "Are you hungry?"

"I'm starving," he said.

Regan adjusted the pillows behind his head, then retrieved the tray and put it in the middle of the bed. "I didn't know what you wanted to drink so I—"

He grabbed the milk and began to gulp it down, then snatched up a piece of bread. "God, this looks good. Did you really cook this?"

Regan watched him settle the bowl of stew on his lap and quickly devour it. He dipped the bread into the gravy and smiled as he chewed. "You could make this every night and I'd eat it."

"I'm sure I can come up with something new. I make really good pasta. And roasted chicken. And meat loaf."

"If it has gravy, I'll eat it. Why don't people eat gravy anymore? I love gravy. This is good gravy."

Regan giggled. "Gravy has gone out of favor with most chefs, I guess."

"My grandmother always used to make it."

"It's comfort food," Regan said.

He nodded, then set his fork down and met her gaze. "This is it," he said softly. "This is how it should be."

"What?"

"Us. You and me. Comfortable. Looking out for each other. Taking care of each other. This is how it's supposed to be, isn't it? This feeling of…contentment."

Regan felt her cheeks warm and she picked up a piece of bread and took a bite. "I—I can't say."

"I'm sure you feel what's between us," Jamie said. "You may not want to admit it yet, but I know you do."

"Just finish your stew," she said.

"Can I have another bowl?"

"You can take mine. I'll go down and get another." She crawled off the bed, then grabbed the empty milk glass. When she reached the hallway, Regan stopped and drew a deep breath.

What was she supposed to feel? And what, exactly, did Jamie want from her? A relationship? A future? It was just beef stew. Of course he was going to feel content. He'd been hungry. She slowly released her breath, moaning softly.

But she'd understood what he'd meant. She'd watched him work himself to near hypothermia over the course of the day, and the moment he stopped, she'd wanted to carry the burden for him. She hadn't thought twice about anything she'd done, from the shower to the supper. She just wanted him warm and safe and comfortable. Was that love? It just seemed so natural, almost instinctual to care about him. Even now, she wondered whether he'd end up with a cold or fever.

She started down the stairs, shaking the thoughts from her head. Maybe she was the one suffering the ill effects of the rain and cold.

"Love is not a bowl of beef stew," she muttered. "I have no idea what it is, but it is certainly not stew."

"I'M A COUPLE days behind," Jamie admitted to his business partners. "But I'm sure I can catch up to the original schedule."

"I'm not so sure," Sam said. "In my opinion, we have two choices. We can show them an incomplete model or we can try to push our meeting back."

Sam and Rick had driven up from Minneapolis that morning, anxious to see the progress on the model house.

Luckily, the rain had stopped and the sun had been out all day, providing good light and warm breezes.

Eddie had arrived at sunrise to take out the trees on the point. Then Cal had arrived with a gas-powered auger that made quick work of digging the holes. By noon, the forms were in the holes and Jamie was mixing concrete. All that was left to do was fire up the forklift and bring the kits over from the other site.

"There is another choice," Rick said. "You can give up this crazy notion that you can build this all on your own. Sam and I are here. Use us. You're ready to put the boxes together, and wrangling those walls will be impossible on your own."

"I knew you'd need another set of hands for that," Sam said.

"I was going to use overhead pulleys," Jamie said. "Or a block and tackle."

"With the three of us, it would take a lot less time and effort."

"But then we can't sell this as a one-man project," Jamie said.

"How many guys would want to build it on their own?" Rick asked. "And the fact is, you *could* build it by yourself. You'd just need a little more time."

"I can do it," Jamie said. "I want to do it."

It really wasn't about the marketing or even setting a goal and reaching it. He wanted to build a home, to know what it felt like to create a space that provided safety and shelter. He hoped it would erase that last tiny bit of fear that he carried with him—the fear of being without a home.

He hadn't realized how much he wanted it until that day in the mud and rain, when everything that could go wrong had seemed to. It had been a metaphor for his childhood, one disaster after another, he and his brothers always on the outside, looking in.

He could buy himself a home. He'd done that already with his condo. But the satisfaction of building one from the ground up was something he'd have for the rest of his life—the knowledge that it wasn't just money and a mortgage that made a home, but hard work and skilled hands.

The cottage was the only home he had. Since selling his condo, he'd been staying with Sam or Rick. Once he was finished here and he told his brothers about his business, he was sure they'd offer a temporary home. But when he needed to be alone, he'd come here.

"Hey, there. How's everything going?"

Regan approached, trudging through the tangle of brush from the beach to the build site. She carried a basket, the handle looped over her arm. Her cheeks were rosy from the chill in the air and her eyes were bright. "It's a beautiful day, isn't it?"

"Much better than rain," Jamie said with a smile. She held out her hand and Jamie grabbed it and helped her up the rise to the cabin site.

Regan brushed a strand of hair out of her eyes and set the basket at her feet. She glanced back and forth between Jamie and his partners.

"Sorry," he murmured. "Sam and Rick, you remember Regan Macintosh."

"Hello," Regan said, shaking their hands.

"How did you get involved in this project?" Sam asked.

"I'm the granddaughter of the landowner. Or lessor, I guess."

"I'm the lessee," Jamie said.

The two men grinned at Jamie, as if they knew exactly what was going on between them. "Right. Lessor and lessee."

"I brought some coffee. And some doughnuts," Regan said. She squatted beside the basket and Jamie bent down next to her. She handed him a box and he grabbed it, then offered a doughnut to the two guests. Mugs of steaming coffee followed before Regan straightened.

"So, what do you think of the progress so far?" she asked.

"He's not going to finish by Monday," Sam said.

"Not if he insists on finishing it himself," Rick added.

Jamie forced a smile. "My partners underestimate my determination."

"I wouldn't do that," Regan said. "When Jamie wants to accomplish something, he doesn't let anything stand in his way. I'd put my money on him if I were you."

"You know, maybe we should get out of here and let you get back to work," Rick said. "If you're going to fit seven days of work into five, you don't have an hour to waste."

"Thanks for the coffee," Sam said. "We'll be back on the weekend if you need help, Jamie. I hope you don't get too distracted by this pretty lady in the meantime."

"Don't worry about the mugs," she said. "You can return them later."

"We'll do that," Sam said.

Jamie walked with them up to the road, reassuring the pair that he had everything under control. "Trust me," he said.

"All right, but we're serious," Rick told him. "If you get in a bind, ask for help. It's not a failing to call in reinforcements. I'm sure the granddaughter would be happy to lend you a hand."

"I think she's got a crush on you," Sam stated.

Jamie chuckled. "Maybe she does. Thanks for offering to help, guys, but there have been people from town hanging around here all day. If I decide I need help, I won't have trouble finding it."

He watched as the two got into Sam's SUV and drove away, then he walked back down to the building site. Regan was sitting on the edge of a floor section, sipping her coffee as she gazed out at the lake.

She turned to look at him as he approached. Regan patted the spot beside her. "Take a break," she said.

He sat down beside her and grabbed a doughnut, then took a big bite. "As you can see, my partners don't have a lot of faith that I can finish the build on time. Is it really that inconceivable that I want to do this on my own?"

"Can you?"

"You believe I can, don't you?"

She smiled. "I'm not exactly an expert at these things."

"But you supported me with Sam and Rick," he said.

"Of course I did. I'll always support you."

"Why?"

"I don't know," she said.

"Yes, you do. It's for the same reason that I'd have your back. And I never thought I needed anyone in this world."

"What do you want from me?" she asked.

"I want what you want," Jamie said.

"Right now what I want is for you to let me help you," she said. "I can do more than take photos. I'm strong and I can use a tape measure and a pencil, which seems to be a big part of this project so far. Oh, and that bubble ruler."

"That's a level," he said.

"Yes. I'm not sure how to use that, but I can learn."

Jamie stared down at her pretty face, at the optimism he saw there. It was just more proof, he mused. They made a good pair. And whatever he might gain by finishing the cabin on his own would be offset by the pleasure of working with Regan.

"Actually, I think it might be fun," she continued. "I could learn to use a power saw. I've always wanted to do that."

"All right," he said. "But you need to promise me one thing. You have to do as I say. No arguments, no complaints."

She gave him a quick salute. "Yes, sir."

He reached in his jacket pocket for a pair of gloves and handed them to her. "They may be a bit big, but you don't want to get any slivers."

"What are we going to do?" she asked.

"I have the floor down. The walls come next."

Before he could move, Regan threw her arms around

his neck and gave him a sweet, deep kiss. When she finally drew back, he smiled at her, brushing a strand of windblown hair from her eyes. "What was that for?"

"For asking me," she said.

Jamie walked her around the site and showed her how the wall sections slipped into a pocket in the floor section. Windows and doors were already cut and hanging in the four-foot-wide sections. The interior structure was made of recycled plastic, insulated for warmth and precut for both plumbing and electricity.

"Let's do this wall first. It fits on the front left corner of that section of floor."

To Jamie's surprise, they installed the first wall module in less than ten minutes, sliding it into place, then screwing it into the base. Another panel followed, neatly fitting into the first.

"They just slide together," she said.

"You only have to secure along the bottom and top. So they can also be disassembled very quickly."

She braced her hands on her waist as she stared at what they'd accomplished. "That looks good. It's nice and straight."

"This whole front wall will be window panels that will overlook the lake," he said. Together, they moved the four panels into place. This time, Regan grabbed the electric driver and placed the screws into the bottom rail.

"I like these long windows. It would be nice to have them open completely so you could just walk out on the deck."

"We have French doors for the other side," he said.

"How are we going to get the roof on?" she asked.

"There are interlocking joists and panels."

"How big will the house be in the end?"

"We'll have one bedroom module with a full bath along with a kitchen module and a living module with a half bath."

"I need to get some photos," she said.

Jamie continued on with the next wall on his own, posing for pictures along the way. Slowly, the cabin was appearing in front of their eyes, nestled among the maples. It didn't seem like work to Jamie. Just a fun activity that they'd decided to do together.

He was beginning to understand how it all happened, how a guy could fall for a girl like Regan and find himself so tangled up in her life that he never wanted to get loose. He watched her as she walked around the site, picking up small bits of garbage.

He didn't care what he had to do to make a future for them—he was willing to do it. He was in charge of sales for Habikit, but as long as he lived near an airport, he'd be fine. He'd make his home wherever she was.

"Let's break for lunch," Jamie said.

"I made some chicken noodle soup," she said.

He grabbed her and gave her a hug. "You're going to make some man a really good girlfriend," he said, kissing the top of her head.

He'd meant it as a joke, but she stiffened beneath his touch. "Or a friend that just happens to be a girl," he added.

Jamie hated this tension that arose every time he mentioned their relationship's status or future. He didn't want to press the issue, but he wasn't going to leave Pickett Lake without a clear understanding of how Regan felt about the two of them.

"NO PEEKING," SHE SAID. "Keep your eyes closed."

Regan opened the door to the new cabin and stepped aside as Jamie entered. It was just past midnight on Sunday night and the cabin was officially finished, on time and under budget.

She'd spent all of Saturday in Minneapolis, shopping for furniture and decor for the interior, while Jamie finished up the last of the siding and roofing. They'd spent early Sunday completing the plumbing and the electricity before Regan had moved in the furniture.

"If you keep my eyes closed much longer, I swear I'm going to fall asleep," Jamie warned.

"Okay," she said. "Open."

Jamie drew his hands away from his eyes and slowly took in the two rooms that held the kitchen, dining and living areas. Regan held her breath, hoping that he'd approve of the eclectic mix of vintage and modern. She'd kept away from the typical north woods decor of bears and pine trees, and instead went for sun-washed colors and a shabby-chic cottage style. It had turned out to be the perfect foil for the simple lines of the modules, and the end result was a clean and comfortable look.

"Wow," Jamie said. "It's—it's…"

"Perfect?" Regan suggested.

He pulled her into a tight embrace. "It is. For the budget I gave you, I'm amazed." He wandered into the kitchen and she held her breath.

She'd fitted out the galley kitchen with vintage appliances from one of her favorite stores in Saint Paul. The old fridge and stove were painted a bright red and contrasted with the soft turquoise she'd chosen for the cabinets and the pale yellow walls.

"I know it's a little strange," she said, "but it will grow on you, I promise."

"I love the vintage appliances." He hugged her again. "And I love you."

Regan's breath caught in her throat. She should have known it was coming. He'd been hinting at it for the past four or five days, pushing her to declare her feelings for him. The problem was, she wasn't sure how deep they ran.

After the disaster with Jake, she couldn't trust her instincts when it came to men. She questioned every feeling she had, every decision she made. So while she admitted she did have feelings for Jamie, how could she be sure they would last?

Regan pushed up on her toes and dropped a quick kiss on his lips. "I'm glad you like it," she said. "I can't believe how fast the cottage went up. You could take your kits into a disaster area and have housing for people within days."

"I have an appointment in Washington, DC, on Wednesday to pitch the idea to FEMA. And then I have to fly out to San Francisco to participate in a symposium on earthquake preparedness. And then I spend the weekend in Chicago."

Regan was shocked. She'd just assumed that after

the cabin was done, Jamie would have some time off, before she had to head to Arizona for her first wedding.

"Why don't you come with me?" Jamie said. "We want to do a presentation with the photos you took, and you could help us. It would be fun—DC, then San Francisco."

"I have a lot of work to catch up on and I have a few photo shoots scheduled for next weekend."

"Then I guess we don't have much time left. I have the investors meeting tomorrow, and after that, I'm going to have to head back to the city."

She reached down and grabbed his hand, then laced her fingers with his. "If we make a plan to see each other and we can't stick to it, we'll only be angry and frustrated. But if we don't have a plan, and we find time to be together, we can never be hurt or disappointed."

"And we'll always be alone," he said. "If I've figured out anything these past few weeks it's that I love being with you. I love waking up with you and falling asleep with you in my arms. I love eating beef stew in bed and washing your hair in the shower."

"I love those things, too," Regan admitted. "But we've had the benefit of being in the exact same place together these past few weeks. We haven't had to deal with physical distance."

"All right," Jamie said. "That could cause a problem. But look at what we did together, Regan. The two people who managed to put this cabin together without killing each other deserve a freaking medal. And a chance to see if they were meant to be together."

"After all you've been through, how is it possible that you still believe in happily-ever-afters?" Regan asked.

"I didn't," Jamie said softly. "Until I met you."

She stepped out of his embrace and slowly walked to the door. "I'm tired. And you have a big day tomorrow. Can we just agree to discuss this at another time?"

"We're running out of other times," he said. He drew a deep breath, then sighed softly, as if he knew it was no use to continue.

She'd told him from the very start that this was only meant to be a short affair, and he'd gladly jumped in. But she'd never, in her wildest dreams, expected him to fall in love with her. Men just didn't do that. When you offered them a way out, they took it.

"Where are you sleeping tonight?" he asked.

She couldn't share his bed in the guest cabin. It was very clear that they had to put distance between them. "I think you should stay in the guest cabin and I'll stay in the lodge. Nana will want to say goodbye to you tomorrow before you leave. Can we plan on lunch at the lodge?"

He nodded. "Thanks for helping me finish the cottage. It was fun."

Regan forced a smile. "It was." She gave him a quick kiss. "I'll see you in the morning."

She opened the door and walked out. A cold wind blew off the lake and a full moon reflected off the water. As she headed for the lodge, Regan turned back to look at the new cottage, still visible through the leafless trees.

Even if she wanted to forget Jamie Quinn, the cottage would be a constant reminder of him and of the time they'd spent together. It was a monument to their short-lived love affair.

Ceci and Cal were still up when she got back to the lodge. They were snuggled together on the sofa, watching an old black-and-white movie. "Darling, I didn't expect to see you tonight," Ceci called.

"We're finished, Nana. At least I am. What are you watching?"

"Roman Holiday," she said. "Audrey Hepburn and Gregory Peck. Come and join us. We just got it started."

"No, it's past midnight. I'm going to bed."

"Past midnight?" Cal said. "How did we lose track of time, Celia? I should get home." He got up and helped Celia to her feet. "Walk me to the door?"

Celia stood and slipped her arm through his. They slowly strolled through the room, then disappeared down the hallway to the front entrance. Regan closed her eyes and listened for the sound of the front door closing. Then she wandered in and joined Celia in the hall, wrapping her arm around her grandmother's waist.

"He's such a good man," Regan said.

"He is," Ceci said. "I thought I was lucky to have one true love in my life, and now I've been blessed with two."

"Will you get married again?"

Ceci turned to the stairs and started to walk up, Regan at her side. "I don't know. We've talked about it, but marriage at our age can complicate things with families and estates. We may just decide to live in sin."

"I doubt anyone would object," Regan said.

"And what about you, darling? What have you and Jamie decided to do?"

"Oh, Nana, we're not so serious. We agreed from the start it wasn't going to amount to anything. It was just a little romance."

"Was it?" Ceci asked. "I've seen the way he looks at you. That is not a man who is ready to give you up."

"He told me he loves me," Regan said.

They'd reached the top of the stairs and Ceci paused. "Well, good for him. The man obviously has some common sense. Of course he loves you. What man wouldn't?"

"Nana, we met less than a month ago. I knew Jake for fifteen years, since I was a kid, and look at what happened. Jamie may say he loves me now, but how can I be sure that's going to last? How can I be sure he won't wake up one day and realize that he made a mistake? Jake loved me and then he didn't."

"No one can be sure of anything in this life, dear. But come on," she said. "Let's both get to bed. Things will look much better in the morning."

"He's leaving tomorrow," Regan said.

"And he'll be back," Ceci said. "Many times."

"Okay, he's leaving *me* tomorrow. It's better this way. We both know exactly where we stand and now we can move on. He'll have a new girlfriend within a month."

Ceci picked Regan's pajamas off the end of the bed and handed them to her, then sat down on the edge of the mattress. "And how would you feel about that?"

"I—I wouldn't care. I ran into Jake the other day at the café and he has a new fiancée. She was really pretty and her name was Kelly and I was perfectly fine with it." It was a bald-faced lie. Regan had been a mess, but after a few days of careful thought, she had felt better.

She changed into her pajamas and crawled into bed, sinking down beneath the covers. She hadn't realized how cold she was until she got out of her clothes and into the warm bed.

Ceci stood up and tucked the covers more tightly around her, then kissed her forehead. "Everything will be clearer in the morning."

"Thanks, Nana. I love you," Regan said.

"I love you, too, darling."

Ceci shut off the lights as she left the room and Regan closed her eyes, pulling the covers up around her face. She'd been awake since sunrise and had spent the entire day working on the cabin. Her body was exhausted, but her mind was filled with thoughts and images.

Regan pulled the pillow over her head and tried to slow her breathing, focusing on the gentle rise and fall of her chest and trying to clear her mind.

She tossed and turned, trying to get comfortable, but nothing seemed to work. She couldn't seem to stop thinking about Jamie. Finally, Regan gave in and let the events of the last few days spin out in her mind.

Images of Jamie drifted in and out. The memory of his voice served as a sedative, weaving a spell around her until she lost touch with reality and found herself caught in a dream.

She felt the bed move and tried to open her eyes. But it was like she was caught in between worlds, waking and dreaming.

"Regan, are you awake?"

He touched her face, and suddenly the spell was broken. She jerked up, searching the dark for anything she recognized.

"Jamie?"

"I'm here," he whispered. His lips touched hers and Regan moaned softly, wrapping her arms around his neck and pulling him close.

"You're here," she said, her fingers smoothing over his face, reading the details in the dark. She dragged back the covers and pulled his naked body into her bed, then curled up against him. He was solid and strong, and she relaxed.

It wasn't right. It didn't fit with what she thought she wanted. But Regan needed him in her bed for just one more night. She'd deal with the consequences in the morning.

9

Two weeks later, Jamie stood at the end of the dock, staring across the lake into the setting sun. In the distance, a power boat skimmed through the water, heading directly for him.

The early November weather had been warm enough to extend the lake season, but there was no doubt that winter was on its way. The trees were bare and the night air was crisp with frost.

"I thought I saw you out here."

Jamie turned to see Celia approach. She was dressed like she had been the very first time he'd met her, in a simple canvas coat and high rubber boots. Her hair, now an attractive platinum blond, was tied back with a colorful scarf. "Hey, Ceci. I was going to stop by to say hello later."

"What are you doing up here?"

He pointed to the boat. "We were getting some shots of the cabin all lit up in the evening light. You can see it perfectly through the trees when you're out on the water. We're going to put it on the cover of a brochure we're making up."

"Good you came today. We're taking the dock out day after tomorrow."

"The season is over," he said. "Pretty soon this whole place will be covered with snow."

The motorboat glided up to the dock, a kid from the boat rental place behind the wheel. Frank Castelle, the commercial photographer that Jamie had hired, leaned over to grab the dock and jumped out of the boat. "I got some terrific shots. High res, really saturated color. I'll have them ready for you in a few days. If you want any changes, let me know."

"I'm sure we'll have a few things we want to tweak," Jamie said. "Thanks for coming out."

"No problem. I'm not going to complain about a few hours on a boat, even if it was a little chilly." The motorboat pulled away from the dock, and Frank waved as he headed for his car.

"Do you have any plans for dinner?" Ceci asked. "I've got a beef stew cooking in the crockpot and no one to share it with."

"Cal isn't here?"

"No, he's on a business trip. He's done some consulting over the years and some company in San Diego needed his help. I was going to go along, but I have family, his and mine, coming for Thanksgiving next week, so I decided I better stay home and get ready."

"I don't have any plans for dinner. And beef stew sounds pretty good right about now."

She slipped her arm around his and they walked up

the rise to the deck and climbed the stairs. Jamie opened the door for her and followed Ceci inside. It had been two weeks since he and Regan had said goodbye to each other, right here, in the kitchen of Ceci's home.

Though he'd pressed her for a commitment, in the end all she could promise was that they'd stay in touch. They had talked three or four times since then. But it wasn't enough, and Jamie felt as though he was losing ground with every phone call.

She'd been offered a job in New York, photographing a bridal gown catalog for a major designer. She'd jetted off just days after they'd said goodbye, so setting a date to meet had been impossible.

"Sit," Ceci said, pointing to the stools along the far edge of the kitchen island. "What can I get you to drink? I have lemonade and beer. Milk and water. I might have a cola."

"How about something stronger," Jamie said. "A whiskey would warm me up."

"I do have whiskey," she said. "Cal enjoys his whiskey, too."

"So how are things going with you and Cal?" Jamie asked.

Ceci retrieved the whiskey from a nearby cabinet, then placed the bottle in front of Jamie. "Ice, water or straight?"

"Straight," Jamie said. She handed him a tumbler and he poured a shot of whiskey into the glass and drank it. The liquor snaked through his bloodstream, warming his limbs along the way.

"Cal and I are just fine. We're so happy and we have so many plans. And I have you to thank for that," Ceci said.

"Me? What did I have to do with it?"

"When I met you that day in the hardware store, I thought you were such an attractive man. Of course, I was old enough to be your grandmother, but it reminded me that I was alive. That I could still get out and enjoy the world and the people in it."

"Is that how you reconnected with Cal?" Jamie asked.

"Yes. Regan helped me get on Facebook and I found Cal, and the rest just happened." She smiled. "Cal and me. You and Regan."

"I'm afraid we haven't had such a happy ending. It's not unhappy. It's just very…vague."

Ceci nodded. "I've tried to talk to her about it, but she can be stubborn. She just doesn't trust herself."

"She doesn't trust me," Jamie said. "She's afraid I'm just going to wake up someday and decide I don't love her. And nothing I've done to this point has been able to change her mind. I don't know what she's looking for."

"She's looking for absolutes," Ceci said. "And she hasn't realized yet that with love, and everything else in life, there are no certainties, no sure things. Someday, she'll be willing to take a risk again."

"I hope it's soon," Jamie said. "I miss her."

"She's coming for Thanksgiving. Why don't you join us?"

Jamie shook his head. He knew exactly how Regan would react if he suddenly showed up at a family function. She didn't want to be pushed, and Jamie was willing to give her some space, at least for a little while. She could have Thanksgiving and Christmas. But he was going to take her out on New Year's Eve. Everyone wanted a date for New Year's Eve, so how could she say no to him?

"I doubt surprising Regan would go over well," he said. "I've got a few plans in mind, though. I haven't given up yet."

"And don't you dare," Ceci warned. "She'll figure out what she wants sooner or later. I'm not sure what it will take, but it will happen, and she'll just snap. Kind of like she did when she met you."

"I'll trust you on that," Jamie said.

Ceci fetched him a bowl of beef stew and set it in front of him. The taste took him back to that night just a few weeks ago, the night he'd realized how good he and Regan were together. He'd been half-frozen and exhausted, and she'd taken care of him. It was the first time he'd ever got a sense of what it might be like to be married—and he'd enjoyed it.

He and his brothers had always avoided deep romantic involvements. They'd all had their own particular reasons for doing so, but lately, Jamie was beginning to acknowledge that such strictly held beliefs could be questioned.

"How is the stew?" Ceci asked.

"Fantastic."

"I'll pack some up for you to take home. If you don't want to drive back tonight, you could always stay. I don't think it would be improper, do you?"

"No, I'd be sure to be a perfect gentleman. But I can't

stay. I have meetings scheduled for tomorrow. And my brother is in town tomorrow night. I'm going to see him play hockey."

"Does he play a lot of hockey?" Ceci asked.

"He used to play for the Blizzard. Then he got traded to New York."

"Your brother is Thom Quinn?" Ceci asked. "My husband used to love him. He was a great fan of the Blizzard. So is Cal. Maybe we can drive down for a game sometime."

"I'd be happy to host you," Jamie said. "Although I'm afraid I'll have to take you out to eat. I'm not much of a cook."

"I want to show you something," Ceci said. "You just finish up your stew. I'll be right back."

Jamie snatched his bowl and added another ladleful of stew, then grabbed a beer from the fridge. He twisted off the cap and took a long sip, then slid back onto his stool.

"I always meant to show you these. I kept photo albums for each of my seventeen grandchildren. All the photos their parents sent me, newspaper clippings, school art projects." She sat down next to Jamie. "This is Regan's."

He glanced over at the bright flowered cover. A photo of a little girl dressed in a white gown and veil was mounted at the center. "Is that Regan?"

"It is."

"At her first communion?"

"Oh, no. That's Halloween. She dressed up as a bride." Ceci opened the book. "Here's another Halloween. Dressed as a bride. And here's another of her just playing dress-up—as a bride." Ceci glanced his way, her eyebrow arched. "From the time she was a very little girl, she's been obsessed with brides. On her tenth birthday, she asked for subscriptions to bridal magazines. Regan used to dress all her dolls in wedding gowns and veils. She spent summers here with us at the lodge and when there was a wedding in town, she grabbed her camera and rode her bike to the church to snap photos of the bride and groom."

"She never told me that," he said. "She said she got interested in wedding photography after going to design school."

"She wanted to learn to design bridal gowns, but she never had much talent for sewing. So she got a degree in commercial design, hoping she could work for one of the bridal magazines. Then her photography took off and that was that."

"I've seen her photos. They seem quite good."

"Yes, she's very much in demand. She did a wedding in France last year. They flew her all the way to Nice and back. Just to take wedding photos."

As Jamie flipped through the photo album, he realized how little he really knew about Regan. Maybe he'd been too optimistic about their future. They'd met just over a month ago. There hadn't been enough time to dig deeper.

"Thank you for showing me this," he said, staring down at a photo from Regan's high school days. She was a beauty then and she still was.

Maybe he didn't know everything about her life and

her past, but he was determined to learn more. And he wanted an entire lifetime to do it. Now all he had to do was convince her that they belonged together.

REGAN PULLED HER bags from the back of the taxi and carefully stacked her camera equipment on top of her carry-on. She hated to drag her equipment on the plane with her, particularly in the middle of January. Which was why she preferred avoiding jumping back and forth between Minneapolis and Arizona.

But her aunt Caroline had planned a Sunday evening anniversary celebration, and of course, she'd been called upon to do the photos. She'd flown in with Ceci, but now she was traveling back to Arizona for another wedding on Friday. Then she'd have to return to Minnesota the following week for a mysterious party that Ceci and Cal were hosting.

She paid the taxi driver and started toward the terminal. The snow had started earlier in the afternoon and was expected to get worse overnight. But the airport was still open, and according to the airline, her flight would leave on time.

Though both Cal and Ceci steadfastly denied it, Regan suspected there might be a wedding in the works. Why else would they throw a big party in the middle of winter? If it were a wedding, than there was a chance Jamie would attend. He had been part of the reason Ceci and Cal were together, after all.

As she walked into the airport, Regan thought about what it might be like to see him again. He'd been back to the model cottage a couple times, but never when she'd been in the area. They'd spoken occasionally on the phone and connected online, but merely to catch up. There was never any talk about their relationship or the future.

And then there had been the New Year's Eve date. He'd called before Christmas to wish her a happy holiday and asked about her plans for the following weekend. Of course, he hadn't known that New Year's Eve was a very popular date for weddings. She'd had a last-minute booking this year that she hadn't hesitated in taking. She'd worked weddings for the last several New Year's Eves, so it'd never occurred to her that she might have a date.

She got in line at the baggage check, and when she reached the desk, she handed the agent her ticket. "I'll check the bag, and then I have these as carry-on," she said, grabbing her bags.

"Sure, but unfortunately, your flight has been delayed for an hour because of the weather," the agent told her.

"I just checked and it was on time."

"They only revised the departure schedules a minute ago. They've gotten behind with deicing the planes. But you should still get out. The heavy snow isn't supposed to start until after midnight."

It would be nice to get off the plane to a warm, breezy night in Phoenix, she thought. Though she loved the change of seasons, Minnesota winters could be so inconvenient—and uncomfortable.

She checked her boarding pass for the gate and decided to get through security and then find something to eat.

"Regan?"

She glanced up to find Jamie standing in front of her. Jamie and a beautiful blonde flight attendant. "Hello," she murmured, her gaze darting back and forth between the two of them.

"I didn't expect to run into you tonight."

"I'm on my way to Arizona. I have a wedding to shoot this weekend, but my flight is delayed because of the snow."

"Is it that bad?" the flight attendant asked. "We just landed."

"It's supposed to get worse," Regan said. She glanced around, then forced a smile. "I should really get going."

"But you said your flight was running late," Jamie said.

"I—I did. I just thought—well, that you probably needed to go."

The flight attendant smiled. "He did promise me dinner," she said. "The best Thai food in town, wasn't it?"

"Have a nice dinner," Regan said. "And it was great to see you again, Jamie. Take care." She turned and hurried down the concourse, determined to put as much distance between them as possible.

Unfortunately, Jamie had other ideas. A few seconds later, he was calling her name again. He fell into step beside her. "What time is your flight leaving?" he asked.

"It was supposed to leave at seven, but it's leaving at about eight now," she said. "Where is your girlfriend?"

"She's not my girlfriend," he said. "I just met her on the plane."

"Still, you made dinner plans," Regan said. "Or did you already forget?"

"No, I haven't forgotten."

"Where is she?"

"She went to her hotel. I told her I wanted to talk to you and I'd catch up with her later. I called you last week, but you never called back."

"I was busy. Why are you following me?"

"I figured we could grab a drink, since you're not leaving for a few hours."

"You're going to take me for drinks and then take another woman to dinner?"

Jamie grabbed her hand and pulled her to a stop. "I'll leave her sitting in the hotel if it means I can spend some time with you. I'm not interested in her. She's just someone I met who wanted to eat Thai food. I was hungry and I thought it would be nice not to have to eat alone."

They reached security and Regan put her camera bags on the belt. She stepped through the metal detector. When he made to follow her, the guard threw an arm out. "You have to have a ticket before you can pass through this checkpoint," the man said.

"Are you really going to make me go back and buy a ticket?" he said to her.

"Go home, Jamie. Or go out to eat with your new friend. But just go."

Regan's heart slammed in her chest and she felt the pressure of tears at the corners of her eyes. She absolutely refused to let him see her in tears.

"All right then. I'll join you in about ten minutes," he called.

She stopped short. She could either talk to him now or in ten minutes. "All right," she said. She walked back past security and stopped in front of him. "Where would you like to go?"

Jamie reached out and grabbed her camera bags, slipping the straps off her shoulders and putting them on his. "There's a nice little bar on the main concourse. Let's go there."

Regan walked beside him, her hands shoved in her jacket pockets, her thoughts focused on what she was going to say to him. She knew from the look on his face that the conversation wasn't going to be light and breezy like their phone conversations.

"I don't want to argue with you," Regan said. "So if this is going to be one long fight, I'd rather leave right now."

Jamie stopped and faced her. "You want to talk it out right here? Fine." He glanced around and spotted a low bench along the wall, then drew her along to it. They sat down together and he set her camera equipment at his feet.

"I got an invitation to some kind of reception at your grandmother's place next week. I know you're going to be there. I don't want it to be uncomfortable. So I'm just going to say some things right now. The first is, I love you, that hasn't changed. I don't have any trouble saying it because I know it's true. I want to spend the rest of my life with you and I don't care if we're married or not, I just want to be with you."

"And the second?" she asked.

"I want to start that life with you right now. I don't care how we make it work. I will do whatever it takes. And third, if you're dead set on rejecting me, I'll understand and move on."

"How would a relationship between us work? You live here and travel around the country promoting Habikit, I bounce back and forth between Arizona and Pickett Lake. I thought your work was important to you."

"It is. And I don't plan to quit anytime soon. But I've been living out of a suitcase long enough to realize that I want a home. And I want someone to come home to. We'll find a way to make it work. We have to, because I don't want to live without you. Here's the thing. Even if we only have a few days a week together, that's a lot better than nothing. And I'm willing to do this on your terms. I want you to be happy."

He stood up and paced back and forth in front of her for a moment. "That's it. I think that's all I have to say." He stopped. "No, there is one more thing. I know I seem like a big risk and I don't have 'marital success' stamped on my forehead. Right now, I don't have a lot of money. But things are definitely looking up. And I will do everything that is humanly possible to make you happy. And I will love you forever." Jamie nodded. "Now that's it. That's all I have to say."

Regan stared up at him, stunned by the raw passion in his plea. Something had changed within her the moment she saw him striding down the concourse with the blonde. And silly as it seemed right now, it had awakened her to feelings that she'd been ignoring for a long time.

Regan drew a deep breath and straightened her spine, ready to tell him how she felt. But he held out his hand, pressing a finger to her lips to silence her.

"Don't," he warned. "I don't want you to respond right now. I want you to let this all simmer for a while. Think about it. Consider everything I've said and then get back to me. In fact, you can tell me at your grandmother's party. You don't even have to say anything. Just ask me to dance and I'll know. If you don't ask me to dance, then it'll be over."

He took a few steps away, then came right back to her. Reaching down, he gently cupped her face in his hands and drew her to her feet. His lips found hers and his kiss was desperate and sweetly delicious, leaving her breathless with desire. He grinned. "Don't forget how good that was between us."

And then he was off, striding down the concourse as if he didn't have a care in the world. Regan tried to catch her breath, but it felt as if someone was trying to smother her. She was hyperventilating and she scrambled to find a solution. A nearby popcorn vendor noticed her distress and handed her an empty bag. She clapped it to her mouth and began to breathe.

Regan felt as if she'd just been run over by a truck, then run over by a bus for good measure. She and Jamie had been apart for two and a half months, and in that time, she'd come to the gradual conclusion that she might have made a mistake in letting him go.

It was clear that he believed she'd made a colossal

mistake, one that might cost her any chance at future happiness, and that if she didn't fix it that very moment, he'd die of a broken heart and she'd be to blame.

She'd been so afraid to risk her heart again, to believe that love could last a lifetime. All her dreams of a perfect wedding had been shattered when Jake had refused to marry her. But those were little-girl dreams and she was a woman now. A woman's dreams were more durable, more flexible. They didn't splinter so easily.

Regan crumpled up the popcorn bag and threw it into the trash, then picked up her camera bags. She'd do as he asked and take her time considering his offer. But she already knew what she wanted. She was ready to take the risk.

Without risk, there would be no reward.

THE PATH TO the model cabin was hidden beneath a fresh coating of snow. Jamie shoved his hands in his jacket pockets and searched for the key to the front door. He wanted to make sure the place was tidy in case anyone at the party might be curious about Habikit's designs and want to see the cottage.

He slipped the key into the lock and opened the door. The place still smelled like fresh lumber and vanilla candles. He walked past a small table and picked up one of the candles Regan had purchased, holding it to his nose. Lavender and vanilla. Her two favorite scents.

Jamie smiled to himself. He did know some things about her. And he learned a little more every time he walked through the model house. He'd come to think of the place as theirs. After all, they'd built it—together.

Regan had decorated it. He'd designed it. And it sat on a piece of land they both loved.

It was odd to think that someday he might have to tear it all apart. The lease agreement ran for only five years. At that point, Regan could choose to buy the place at a negotiated price or he would tear it down.

He walked through the house, switching on the lights as he moved from room to room. Jamie loved the view of the water from the kitchen, though the lake was frozen now. Maybe later he'd take a walk on the ice.

"Hello? Anybody home?"

Jamie climbed the stairs to the main level and found Sam standing at the wide wall of windows. "Sam. What are you doing here?"

"I was invited," he said.

Rick stepped through the front door, brushing the snow off his jacket. "Me, too. What's going on?"

"I don't know. I assumed Cal and Ceci had organized a reception because they'd decided to get married. But I'm not sure why they'd invite you."

"Ceci owns the big house?" Sam asked.

He nodded. "Listen, I'm going to see if I can figure out what's happening. I just wanted to make sure this place looked ready to show."

"Good idea," Rick said. "We'll follow you up to the lodge after we turn off all the lights."

Jamie headed back outside, then followed the path up to the road. He walked along the line of cars parked on either side. The driveway to the lodge had been plowed and salted, making it easier for guests hurrying into the party.

From outside, he could hear the sound of music, but when he entered and started circulating, he realized it was coming from speakers tucked discreetly around each room. He recognized the tune and whistled along with it softly as he searched the lodge for a singular face.

Jamie first saw her from across the great room. She was standing near the fireplace, a glass of champagne clutched in fingers. He watched as she took a sip, then scanned the room.

Was she looking for him? He'd been a half hour late, trying to find a place to park along the snowbound road above the lodge, and then checking on the model home. Jamie grabbed a flute of champagne from a passing waitress. She gave him a coy smile, one that telegraphed her interest. In a few minutes, she'd find him, this time with a tray of hors d'oeuvres and a phone number.

It was a game he'd played for many years, but he had no interest in it anymore. He didn't return the girl's smile. His gaze came to rest on Ceci and Cal, the pair holding court along the wall of windows. Ceci was dressed in a beaded tunic and a long satin skirt. He caught her eye and waved at her, and she sent him a brilliant smile.

The place looked beautiful, decorated with tiny white lights and lush bouquets of white flowers—roses and lilies and another flower that one of the ladies called stock. Candles were scattered all around, adding to the romantic ambience.

Most of the guests were expecting a wedding, but now Jamie had his doubts. Celia hadn't given him any indication that she and Cal planned to marry, but what else could bring such a diverse crowd together? There were people from town, family members, and oddest of all, Jamie's two business partners.

He stayed in the shadows, watching Regan. She wore a knit dress that clung to every curve of her body, from her breasts to her tiny waist to the sweet curve of her hips. The eggplant color was a perfect complement to her pale skin. Her hair was its usual tousled mess, but this time the style seemed more deliberate.

She spotted his business partners and wandered over to them. When they walked outside onto the deck, he took the chance to say hello to Ceci and Cal.

"Looks like a great party," Jamie said.

"There you are!" Ceci said. "We've been waiting for you to come and say hello. I've seen you slinking around the perimeter of the room."

"Me? You don't need me to throw a good party."

"We need you for this one," Cal said.

"What are we all doing here?" Jamie asked. "It's not your wedding. I'm pretty sure it's not *my* wedding. I hope to hell it's not Regan's wedding."

Cal turned to Ceci. "Are you ready, sweetheart?" He took her hand and led her through the crush of guests, then helped her to stand on the stone hearth.

"Can someone call in the guests from the deck? I have an announcement to make."

Regan wandered back in with Rick and Sam. She caught sight of Jamie almost immediately and their gazes locked for a long moment before other guests blocked their view.

"Ladies and gentlemen, dear friends and family, there's been a lot of speculation about why we've brought you all together, and let me assure you right now, it is not for a wedding."

A disappointed groan rose from the crowd and Ceci shushed them. "If I ever decide to get married again, you will all get a proper invitation and I'll expect a proper wedding gift."

This brought a round of laughter and applause.

"A few months ago, I made the acquaintance of a very interesting young man," Ceci continued. "His name is James Quinn and he'd standing right here, in front of me."

Jamie frowned. What was this all about? He slowly turned to face the crowd and found them all watching him with blatant curiosity.

"Jamie and his business partners had an extraordinary plan to provide housing for the homeless. Tiny structures with small kitchens and baths, quick to build, easy to move and using recycled materials to make each little home affordable. My granddaughter Regan was also impressed. Regan, why don't you join us? You're part of this story, too."

When she got to Jamie's side, he leaned closer. "Do you know what this is about?"

"No. But if it gets embarrassing, promise me you'll get me out of here."

He took her hand and gave it a squeeze. "Promise."

Ceci went on to tell the story of the model cottage and how she'd watched the working relationship between Regan and Jamie evolve.

"I must say, something about this project sparked my imagination. Of course, you all know that Cal and I have both been very fortunate in our lives, and we both felt it was time to give back. So we've set up a foundation that will provide funds to Jamie's company, Habikit, and put these wonderful little houses into cities all over the country. We plan to set up small communities on land we purchase, and provide a safe, comfortable and secure way for homeless individuals to maintain their independence while they get back on their feet."

The guests clapped and cheered, and Jamie glanced over at Regan. "This is not what I was expecting," he murmured.

"Of course, Cal and I will serve on the board of trustees," Ceci continued.

"Ceci will be our president," Cal said.

"And we'll be hiring a small staff. We've already found an executive director. And tonight, we are naming Regan and Jamie to our board of trustees. I think that between the two of them, they will see that our money is well spent." Ceci pulled out a cardboard check and handed it to Jamie. "This is a check for two hundred fifty thousand dollars, to replace the one that Regan ripped up. And this is another check to purchase property and thirty homes for the Twin Cities Homeless Project."

The party guests erupted in enthusiastic applause. Jamie glanced down at Regan and saw the stunned look on her face. He gave her hand another squeeze. As a crowd of guests surrounded Ceci and Cal, offering donations to the project, Sam and Rick hurried up to Jamie.

"Did you know about this?" Sam asked.

Jamie shook his head. "Not a clue. This is going to get us off to a good start."

"We're going to take anyone who is interested on a tour of the cottage. Good thing we already opened it up," Rick said. He turned to Regan. "Thank you. I'm sure you had something to do with this."

"I didn't," Regan said. "It was all my grandmother—and Cal."

Jamie pulled Regan through the crowd toward the foyer. "So, it looks like we're going to be seeing more of each other," he said.

"Leave it to Nana to find a way. The woman never gives up. I pity her friends when she starts fund-raising. She is relentless."

"Come with me." Jamie led her through the celebrating guests and into the hallway, then up the stairs to the second floor. Some of the guests had also wandered upstairs, but the bedroom at the end of the hall was empty. He pulled her inside and locked the door behind him.

"What are you doing?"

"There's no room for dancing downstairs."

"I'm sure there will be when people get drunk enough," she said.

Jamie pulled his phone from his pocket and searched his music library for a suitable song. The strains of a big-band version of "When I Fall in Love" came through the tiny speakers. He tucked the phone into his palm and turned to her.

"It's time for you to decide," Jamie said. "Are we going to dance or what?"

"I have to decide? Just like that?"

He nodded. "It's simple. Just hold out your hand and I'll take it. You don't even have to say a word."

Regan lifted her hand, but her fingers trembled and she quickly clasped them to her chest. "I don't know if I can do this."

"Trust me," Jamie whispered. "I promise, I will love you until the end of time."

She drew a deep breath and took a step closer. "It has to be forever."

Jamie nodded again. "Forever. I promise."

A tiny smile quirked at the corners of her mouth. "Jamie Quinn, will you dance with me?"

He let out a tightly held breath and clasped her hand, then drew her against his body. His right hand slid around her waist and came to rest on the small of her back. His left hand held her fingers and his phone. "I would love to dance," he said.

Slowly, they began to sway to the music. Though he'd always known Regan to be an incredibly strong woman, at that moment she seemed completely vulnerable. He would protect this woman with his life, because she *was* his life.

"Do we get to live happily ever after now?" Regan asked.

"I think we do," he said. "Starting right now."

He danced her across the room and back again, pausing to twirl her beneath his arm. "Have I told you how beautiful you are tonight?" he asked.

"I don't believe you have," she said, her eyes alight with humor.

"My dear, you're not just beautiful, you're also lovely and stunning. And I'm definitely a fan of this dress." He smoothed his hand from her waist to her hip, then around to the small of her back. From what he could tell, she wasn't wearing panties, a fact that intrigued him.

"I know exactly what you're thinking," she said.

"No, you don't."

"I do. You're wondering if I'm wearing underwear."

"Beautiful and clairvoyant," he said. "And what am I thinking now?"

"You're wondering how long it will take me to get out of this dress."

"No, that's not it at all. I was just thinking that we really should get a picture of this. This is one of those moments you don't want to forget. Would you like to do the honors?"

Regan took his phone and aimed the camera at them both, and they smiled as she pressed the button. Then she turned and checked the screen, holding it out for him to see.

"They look very happy, don't they?" he said. "He looks like he's in love."

"So does she," Regan said softly. "This might be the most perfect picture I've ever taken."

He spun her around, then picked her up off her feet. "You may be right."

Epilogue

THE MONDAY NIGHT crowd at O'Malley's Pub had turned boisterous in the after-dinner hours. Outside, snow had begun to fall, thick flakes quickly covering the cars and giving the patrons a reason to stay a little longer.

"All right, all right," shouted Jimmy, the bartender. He stood up on a step stool at the end of the bar and motioned for the crowd to be quiet. "This here's a public service announcement for every bowser, dickweed and gobshite who might be drinking with us tonight. I'll remind you that tomorrow is Valentine's Day and if you haven't yet bought your wife, your girlfriend or both a gift, Jimmy has these lovely boxes of bonbons for sale at a reasonable price. Don't be caught out in the cold, gents."

Jamie chuckled softly. He couldn't remember the last time he'd celebrated Valentine's Day. Third or fourth grade, perhaps? It had always been one of those holidays that other people found important, for no good reason. Who could be silly enough to believe in a naked nymph with a bow and arrow who would make all your romantic dreams come true?

The holiday was tomorrow and he still wasn't sure how he was going to celebrate it, or what he was going to buy Regan as a gift. Given his choice, he was ready to give her an engagement ring, but she was still insisting that there was no reason at all for the two of them to get married.

The bartender set two pints in front of him and Jamie reached for his wallet. But his brother Tris dropped his credit card on the bar first. "I'll get the first round. Thom can get everything after that. He's the one making all the money."

Tris picked up a pair of red sunglasses with two googly, heart-shaped eyes on springs. "This is exactly how I feel when I see Lily," he said. "I might have to get these. She would find them amusing."

"That's exactly how every woman looked when they saw those nude paintings she did of you."

"Yeah? No wonder. Lily was very generous when it came to my genitalia. It's a good quality to have in a mate."

"Lucky you," Jamie muttered.

It was odd to talk to his brothers about women. Not that they hadn't in the past, but it had always been in general terms. Girls were gross, girls were stupid, girls were the most fascinating creatures on the planet.

Now, the women had names and faces. Thom was involved with Malin Pedersen, the daughter of the Blizzard team owner, and the woman responsible for bringing him back to the Twin Cities to play hockey.

Tris had been living with Lily Harrison, an artist and poet and the daughter of a wealthy Minneapolis industrialist. And now, the youngest brother had finally found his match. He hadn't told his brothers yet, but he'd introduce them all to Regan at the next Sunday dinner with their grandmother.

"Have you bought a present for Lily? Isn't this the most important holiday of the year when it comes to romance?"

Tristan shrugged. "Lily doesn't like to follow standard protocol when it comes to these things. She thinks Valentine's Day is just a way for the card companies to make millions of dollars to feed their greedy investors, all at the expense of the romantic ideals of Western civilization. I heard her whole rant on it last night. She made me promise I wasn't going to buy her anything."

"So you lucked out," Jamie said.

"No."

Tris reached in his pocket and pulled out a small velvet box.

"You bought her an engagement ring?"

"Try again. She feels the same way about the diamond industry as she does about the greeting card industry." Tris opened the box. "I got her this. It's a diamond-and-onyx pin. Set in platinum. Art deco. It once belonged to Isadora Duncan."

"You bought her used jewelry?"

"No! Isadora was a dancer. She's one of Lily's idols. She's going to love it."

"Going to love what?"

Thom slid onto the stool next to Tris, leaning in to

examine Tris's gift. "Nice," he said. "You can never go wrong with a tie clasp. They're back in now."

"It's a pin," Tris said. "For Lily. For Valentine's Day."

Thom grinned. "Like I said, you can never go wrong with one of the big three."

"What are the big three?" Jamie asked.

"Jewelry, flowers, candy."

"And what did you get Malin?" Jamie inquired.

"That's between the two of us," Thom said, motioning to the bartender.

Tris began to lecture him about his penchant for keeping secrets, and Thom finally gave in and reached into his pocket. "This is a very complicated gift," he said, bringing out a bag.

"Those look like M&Ms," Tris said.

"They are. Malin has been craving chocolate lately and the only thing that seems to satisfy her are red M&Ms."

Jamie picked up the package and examined the candy through the clear plastic. "These are pink. And there's a picture of someone's face on the candy."

"Yeah, that's the funny part. You can get anything printed on these. So I had a buddy use one of those apps that combines two faces into one, where they take a picture of a man and a woman and put them together to show you what your kid will look like. That's it. That's our kid."

"And you put that on a piece of candy?"

"Yeah," Thom said. "Although I guess it makes more sense if you know that Malin is pregnant. We're going to have a baby girl."

The shock of Thom's announcement brought a gasp from both Jamie and Tris, but once they'd caught their breath, they congratulated him, patting him on the back and ordering up shots of whiskey for the entire bar to toast the good news.

"With all this happy news from the two of us, it's sad to know that our little brother is going to spend his Valentine's Day all alone," Tris said, giving Jamie a small shove. "We could at least try to find him a date."

Jamie smiled. After Thom's big news, telling them about Regan shouldn't cause a bigger fuss. "You don't have to worry. I have a date for Valentine's Day. I'm flying down to Scottsdale tomorrow and spending the next week with her."

"Her?"

"Her name is Regan Macintosh. She's a wedding photographer. And I'm pretty much madly in love with her. And have been since I met her in October."

"And what are you getting her for Valentine's Day?" Thom asked. "It better be good."

"She won't actually get the present until next spring. But I bought her flowers," Jamie said.

"You're supposed to get the flowers on Valentine's Day," Tris said.

"Actually, they're not flowers yet. I bought bags and bags of daffodil bulbs. I had a landscaper plant them in the woods around the model house. It's technically her property, but I thought it would be cool if, every spring, the entire woods were filled with flowers."

Tris nodded. "Not bad."

"I like it," Thom said.

"Unless the deer dig them up and eat them," Tris added.

"So, I guess we're all set," Jamie said. "The three Quinn brothers have finally got it all figured out. There is a happy ending if you're patient."

Thom ordered another round of shots for the three of them and held up his shot glass. "To happy endings," he said.

They touched the glasses together and Jamie downed the shot in one gulp. A happy ending. He couldn't ask for anything more.

* * * * *

REQUEST YOUR FREE BOOKS!
2 FREE NOVELS PLUS 2 FREE GIFTS!

red-hot reads!

YES! Please send me 2 FREE Harlequin® Blaze® novels and my 2 FREE gifts (gifts are worth about $10). After receiving them, if I don't wish to receive any more books, I can return the shipping statement marked "cancel." If I don't cancel, I will receive 4 brand-new novels every month and be billed just $4.74 per book in the U.S. or $5.21 per book in Canada. That's a savings of at least 14% off the cover price. It's quite a bargain. Shipping and handling is just 50¢ per book in the U.S. and 75¢ per book in Canada.* I understand that accepting the 2 free books and gifts places me under no obligation to buy anything. I can always return a shipment and cancel at any time. Even if I never buy another book, the two free books and gifts are mine to keep forever.

150/350 HDN GH2D

Name _____
(PLEASE PRINT)

Address _____ Apt. # _____

City _____ State/Prov. _____ Zip/Postal Code _____

Signature (if under 18, a parent or guardian must sign) _____

Mail to the **Reader Service:**
IN U.S.A.: P.O. Box 1867, Buffalo, NY 14240-1867
IN CANADA: P.O. Box 609, Fort Erie, Ontario L2A 5X3

Want to try two free books from another line?
Call 1-800-873-8635 or visit www.ReaderService.com.

* Terms and prices subject to change without notice. Prices do not include applicable taxes. Sales tax applicable in N.Y. Canadian residents will be charged applicable taxes. Offer not valid in Quebec. This offer is limited to one order per household. Not valid for current subscribers to Harlequin Blaze books. All orders subject to credit approval. Credit or debit balances in a customer's account(s) may be offset by any other outstanding balance owed by or to the customer. Please allow 4 to 6 weeks for delivery. Offer available while quantities last.

Your Privacy—The Reader Service is committed to protecting your privacy. Our Privacy Policy is available online at www.ReaderService.com or upon request from the Reader Service.

We make a portion of our mailing list available to reputable third parties that offer products we believe may interest you. If you prefer that we not exchange your name with third parties, or if you wish to clarify or modify your communication preferences, please visit us at www.ReaderService.com/consumerschoice or write to us at Reader Service Preference Service, P.O. Box 9062, Buffalo, NY 14240-9062. Include your complete name and address.

Hannah Hastings is just looking for a hot vacation fling.
Can fun-loving and downright gorgeous rancher
Seth Landers tempt her to stay forever?

Read on for a sneak preview of
SIZZLING SUMMER NIGHTS,
the latest book in Debbi Rawlins's much loved
***MADE IN MONTANA** miniseries.*

"I think the best we can hope for is no rocks." Seth nodded to an area where the grass had been flattened.

"This is fine with me," she said, and helped him spread the blanket. "What? No pillows?"

Seth chuckled. "You've lived in Dallas too long."

Crouching, he flattened more of the grass before smoothing the blanket over it. "Here's your pillow, princess."

Hannah laughed. "I was joking," she said, then pinned him with a mock glare. "Princess? Ha. Far from it."

"Come here."

"Don't you mean, come here, please?" She watched a shadow cross his face and realized a cloud had passed over the moon. It made him look a little dangerous, certainly mysterious and too damn sexy. He could've just snapped his fingers and she would've scurried over.

"Please," he said.

She gave a final tug on the blanket, buying herself a few seconds to calm down. "Where do you want me?"

HBEXP0217

"Right here." He caught her arm and gently pulled her closer, then turned her around and put a hand on her shoulder. "Now, look up. How's this view?"

Hannah felt his heat against her back, the steady presence of his palm cupping her shoulder. "Perfect," she whispered.

His warm breath tickled the side of her neck. He pressed his lips against her skin. "You smell good," he murmured, running his hand down her arm. With his other hand he swept the hair away from her neck. His breath stirred the loose strands at the side of her face.

Hannah was too dizzy to think of one damn thing to say. She saw a pair of eerie, yellowish eyes in the trees, low to the ground. Then a howl split the night. She stifled a shriek, whirled and threw her arms around Seth's neck.

He enfolded her in his strong, muscled arms and held her close. "It's nowhere near us."

"I don't know why it made me jumpy," she said, embarrassed but loving the feel of his hard body flush with hers. "I'm used to coyotes."

"That was a wolf."

Wolf? Did they run from humans or put them on the menu? She leaned back and looked up at him. Before she could question whether or not this was a good idea, Seth lowered his head.

Their lips touched and she was lost in the fog.

Don't miss
SIZZLING SUMMER NIGHTS
by Debbi Rawlins, available March 2017 wherever
Harlequin® Blaze® books and ebooks are sold.

www.Harlequin.com

HBEXP0217

SPECIAL EXCERPT FROM

HQN™

Single mom Harper Maclean has two priorities—raising her son and starting over. Her mysterious new neighbor is charming and sexy, but Diego Torres asks far too many questions…

*Enjoy a sneak peek of CALL TO HONOR, the first book in the new **SEAL BROTHERHOOD** series by Tawny Weber.*

Harper stepped outside and froze.

Diego was in his backyard. Barefoot and shirtless, he wore what looked like black pajama bottoms. Kicks, turns, chops and punches flowed in a seamlessly elegant dance.

Shirtless.

She couldn't quite get past that one particular point. But instead of licking her lips, Harper clenched her fists.

She watched him do some sort of flip, feet in the air and his body resting on one hand. Muscles rippled, but he wasn't even breathing hard as he executed an elegant somersault to land feet first on the grass.

Wow.

He had tattoos.

Again, wow.

He had a cross riding low on his hip and something tribal circling his biceps.

Who knew tattoos were so sexy?

Harper's mouth went dry. Her libido, eight years in deep freeze, exploded into lusty flames.

The man was incredible.

Short black hair spiked here and there over a face made for appreciative sighs. Thick brows arched over deep-set eyes, and he had a scar on his chin that glowed in the moonlight.

Harper decided that she'd better get the hell out of there.

But just as she turned to go, she spotted Nathan's baseball.

"You looking for the ball?" His words came low and easy like his smile.

"Yes, my son lost it." She eyed the distance between her and the ball. It wasn't far, but she'd have to skirt awfully close to the man.

"Good yard for working out," he said with a nod of approval. He grabbed the ball, then stopped a couple of feet from her.

"I should get that to Nathan." She cleared her throat, tried a smile. "He's very attached to it."

"The kid's a pistol." His eyes were much too intense as he watched her face.

That's when she realized what she must look like. She'd tossed an oversize T-shirt atop her green yoga bra and leggings. Her hair was pulled into a sloppy ponytail, and she wore no makeup.

"Thanks for finding it."

His eyes not leaving hers, he moved closer.

Close enough that his scent—fresh male with a hint of earthy sweat and clean soap—wrapped around her.

Finally, he placed the ball in her outstretched hand. "Everything okay?"

No. Unable to resist, she said, "Why do you ask?"

"I don't like seeing a beautiful woman in a hurry to get away from me." The shadows did nothing to hide the wicked charm of his smile or the hint of sexual heat in his gaze.

It was the same heat Harper felt sizzling deep in her belly.

Thankfully, the tiny voice in her mind still had enough control to scream, "Danger."

"I'm hurrying because I don't like to leave my son inside alone," she managed to say. "Again, thanks for your help."

And with that, she slipped through the hedge before he could say another word. It wasn't until she was inside the house that she realized she was holding her breath.

What's next in store for Harper, Diego and the SEAL Brotherhood? Find out when CALL TO HONOR *by* New York Times *bestselling author Tawny Weber, goes on sale in February 2017.*